Southern Cross

Southern Cross

By

Janet Faulk

Artwork by Benjamin Blanchard

Cover design by Martin W. Romero

ISBN: 978-0-9997804-2-8

Library of Congress Control Number: 2018960041

This book is dedicated with gratitude:
to my dear friends Diane M. Moore and Victoria Sullivan who have been
with me, with a hand at my back, for the 10 years it took me to write this story
and the years before when the seed of the story was a newspaper article in a
folder that I couldn't stop talking about;

to the unnamed diarist from the Gulf Coast who captured my
imagination;

to my son Benjamin Blanchard with whom I am always joyful to have a
creative collaboration;

to my brother Craig A. Faulk who believed in my effort enough to build a
writing desk for me;

and to my husband Rudolfo Valentine Gonzales, my own Valentine, who
made me many Saturday breakfasts so that I could squeeze in time to quilt
these words together.

Out beyond ideas of wrongdoing and right doing,
there's a field. I'll meet you there. When the soul lies down in that
grass,
the world is too full to talk about.
Ideas, language, even the phrase *each other*
doesn't make any sense
—Rumi—

TABLE OF CONTENTS

The Story Behind the Story

Struggle with a sense of place has loomed heavy in my psyche as long as I can remember. I don't know how other stories come about, but this one was given to me, and its importance confirmed year after year until the task of writing it was at least somewhat complete. I am grateful that the story chose me; writing it has been one of the most important journeys in my life. Messages were provided all along the way that I should not give up; I never tired of effort.

The seed of the story was planted in 1997 when visiting my family in Alabama, I picked up the August 24 edition of the *Eufaula Tribune* and read the article by Ann S. Smith, *"Brazilian Finds Roots Here."* Thirteen years later I began writing the story, and that is what I labeled it for years, "the story."

The Internet is an incredible source of information and surprise. From time to time I searched for diaries of southerners who may have made the journey described in the story. Finally, one evening in 2009, one appeared. *"Brazilian Travel Diary, 1866, Collection Number 5235-z"*. Deepest appreciation to the librarian who had the journal scanned and sent to me on compact disc. I spent well over a year endeavoring to read the long-hand journal of the man who made the voyage and who never once referenced himself or his family by name. He provided the story with an authenticity that it would never have had otherwise. Of great interest to me is the fact that this journal was housed in the Manuscripts Department of Wilson Library on the University of North Carolina campus, which was the location of my very first job out of college. I have learned that the university did not purchase the journal until 2005, so it was not there when I was there, but still, you can appreciate the link.

I have done a tremendous amount of research for this story, but a fiction story remains one person's perception. I generally endeavored to be as accurate as possible with details historically relevant to the time and places; however, I will admit that there are times when I shifted a few years here or there to make the story work. Only once did I willfully choose an unauthentic detail, which happens to be the appearance of a Blue Tick Coonhound.

I recognize the works of Zora Neal Hurston and Sylviane A. Diouf which gave me new awareness and understanding of the African slave trade. Just days after losing a potential local contact that could help me with some details of the story, I learned that Zora Neal Hurston's book *Barracoon* was going to be released within weeks. It was exactly what I needed.

I acknowledge my friend and colleague Kelly N. Roark for helping to keep me on track regarding the Choctaw characters, and most recently, to Sandra Medlock, Operations Manager, Mississippi Band of Choctaw Indians, who showed up at the perfect moment to help me with some terminology. It's been like that all along the way—what I've needed has turned up.

And finally, I would like to thank the jeweler who made the necklace that appears in the story. She has no idea I exist, but through her artwork, Christine DesJardins provided me with the ending to the story. Thank you, Edie Casselman, for encouraging me to "buy the necklace" and for the time you spent with me as the story unfolded.

I am sure that I have not done any group or subgroup that appears in the story true justice, but perhaps the story will inspire someone else to take a closer look. It has been a healing journey for me.

1866

Near the Escatawpa River, Mississippi
August 1865

As Kate came across the open, dry field up the rise from the banks of the Escatawpa River, she noticed every indication that August gave her of this familiar place — tiny bluebell flowers, red-seeded grass and the smell of honeysuckle. She reached for the tender yellow trumpet bloom and easily pulled the nectar from its throat, thinking it remarkable that while everything changes, some things remain the same. She cradled her tongue and held the honeysuckle's sweetness there until it melted in her warm mouth.

Standing as still as the dry grass itself, with only the wide-brim of her shabby straw hat to shield her face from the mid-morning sun, she pulled several more blooms, acutely aware of her own presence, enjoying each drop of the nectar, before gathering up her faded cotton skirt on the side, and tucking the hem in her waistband, exposing her white thigh and Brogans. As she turned to head back up the sloping field to the house, she noticed a slender coach whip slither in the opposite direction. In an earlier time, she would've been panicked by proximity to a snake, but either she'd become braver over the years or maybe was just less surprised by anything life presented.

To remove some of the dust from her heavy shoes, she stomped her feet on the weathered steps that folded out from the wide porch and spilled into the sandy shaded yard, which within a short distance ran beneath the live oaks, then stretched itself into acres of open grassland bordered by split rail fencing. Kate looked around at the place where she'd lived for the past seven years or so and found it oddly unfamiliar. She'd moved to the Thompson farm just before her 29 birthday when she'd married Jake Thompson and before the world, as she knew it, began to fall apart.

Having so much time for contemplation might have been a luxury at some time in the past, but there were days when she could conjure no vision of her future and wasn't sure how to begin thinking through what her next course of action might be. She didn't hear the mosquito buzzing around her head but noticed it only when it landed on the back of her hand; its thin legs like the single stroke of a graphite pencil. She noticed, for the first time, the tiny white dots over the mosquito's body and became preoccupied with its sheer weightlessness as it began to drill into her hand. She wondered at how such a slight thing had the power to pierce her skin and cause such immediate misery. Unwilling to suffer the consequence of continued observation, she instinctively swatted it, leaving a bloody smear. She held on to the moment long enough to be frustrated by the bothersome mosquito so early in the morning.

Kate made her supper of warm tomato gravy by lighting the small fire pit she'd created behind the house. It used less wood than the stove, and since she was only cooking for herself, it didn't make much sense to use firewood so frivolously. It was a major task now for her to chop the wood, and she never wanted her neighbors around the bend to feel obligated to supply her lighter'd and fire logs. She'd learned to use the heart of the yellow pines that had been cut in the spring because the bark rots around it but the heart of the pine stays solid as if it were a hardwood tree. She chopped out pieces about three feet long and split them into sections about an inch square. These made good starter pieces for the fire. Her mind drifted to a vague memory of her grandfather making torches from the heart of tall pine stumps for hunting possums at night, but quickly her thoughts returned to the task at hand as she retrieved a little fat that she stored cool by hanging it, wrapped in gauzy linen-like cloth, down the well. When the fat began to sizzle, she threw in a slight handful of precious flour, constantly stirring until it was lightly browned. Then, she added the over-ripe tomatoes she'd peeled and mashed. It had been a good year for her garden yield, especially for the juicy almost sweet tomatoes. She blended these ingredients, sprinkling in ground rosemary that grew near the edge of the porch as salt and black pepper were virtually nonexistent. She let the mixture simmer a bit, moving the heavy two-inch deep, cast iron frying pan on and off the fire to keep a low simmer that would prevent the flour from sticking and burning. She split a biscuit left over from a day or so ago and poured the warm tomato gravy on top.

Kate reached for the glass of water that she'd dipped from the bucket she kept dangling above the well and took her supper around to the front steps to watch the sunset. She'd lost interest in eating alone at the table even though it would've created some sense of normalcy. She had come to prefer what suited her needs above what she thought the expectation might be. She wasn't even sure who was doing the "expecting" anymore. She'd stopped juggling her choices regarding normalcy weeks before.

Finishing her supper, she took a small corner of the biscuit that she intentionally kept gravy-less and smeared it with golden scuppernong jelly—a real treat. As she watched the lingering sunset shrouding the western sky a pulpy peach, she exhaled another day and inhaled hope for what tomorrow might bring.

Kate Teal realized she was waiting for disapproving tones disallowing her consideration for leaving. She realized that this admonishment was why she'd been waiting. She'd come to her decision days, even weeks ago, but she was waiting for something and didn't know what until today. She'd been waiting all this time for someone to tell her she couldn't go. She'd been waiting to defend herself against the fears that her husband, father-in-law, mother, sister, her father would've had, but over the years these people were removed from her in one way or another, and their voices had become nothing more than whispers in the faint evening light.

She knew she'd still face resistance from the world at large. She wasn't so worried about that. The social infrastructure of her world had crumbled under the weight of war just like the economy. People were too busy walking around in disbelief or trying to reconstruct their own family to worry too much about the decisions of one woman. She saw now that there might be newfound personal freedom in the distraction. If she thought very long about this possibility of freedom it might be frightening, so with a deep sigh, she let the thought go like dry leaves in a warm autumn breeze.

Nothing brings buried thoughts to the surface like the first dark of evening. At twilight when shadows lay long and thin in the grass, the fading light of day pulls color along with it and orchestrates a symphony of evening sound. This is the time of day when it becomes difficult to tell a black cat from its shadow and stillness spills over the earth like indigo ink. Then, the night movement takes shape with the subtle rustle of a raccoon family easing along the water's edge, the whirr of seven-year locusts creating a rhythmic background for an occasional bullfrog croaking and the singular intermittent chirping of a lone cricket.

On this evening, Kate sat on the steps with her knees drawn up to her chest and arms wrapped around them so that her chin rested on the tops of her knees. She sat in the early evening with full awareness that even though her life wasn't what she'd expected it to be, it wasn't over. The remainder of her journey would come to her, just as the events of the earlier years had presented themselves in their own good time. She knew that the moment didn't call for apathy or whining, but patience with herself, even though having patience with herself wasn't her strong suit. This intuition calmed her and gave her the strength to watch for an opportunity that might be about to present itself.

Kate had always been a solitary soul, often choosing domestic activities like spinning or blackberry picking that moved her away from the social quilting circles and afternoon teas with which her time could've been filled. It wasn't that she didn't like people, quite the contrary, but she found social occasions filled with distractions that prevented her from genuinely knowing people and a waste of time.

These last few weeks, she'd come to feel more alone than she'd felt before. The Bowman's, distant relatives and her neighbors across the way were joining up with a group out of Mobile and heading west, maybe to east Texas, which had some similarities to western Mississippi or perhaps to a place called Tucson in the Arizona Territory.

Custom practically forbade it and conditions weren't favorable for a woman to live alone, but she simply had not decided that this was the best move for her and was stubborn enough to resist traveling with the Bowmans. She loved them all; they'd indeed become her family, but it wasn't the best option for her, an answer that she couldn't even explain to herself. She must have sounded like a reckless fool to them all, but she had to ignore those concerns and stand solidly on her belief that she could trust no one with her future but herself.

Since she was a slight, freckle-faced girl, Kate stood watching the world from a distance. Living its inconsistencies, she'd spent her life looking for the kernel of truth that kept an idea honest, watching for a place of understanding and compromise, listening for evidence that would rectify the misguided and misunderstood; but this was more than she could manage, so even though she wasn't exactly sure how yet, she knew she'd leave this place with no expectation of returning. She did, however, require herself to believe, with all earnestness, that her decision was taking her towards something rather than away from something. In that very moment, she made a firm and conscious decision to move forward, towards something, even if she didn't know what it was.

Kate had grieved the loss of her young husband. To lose him so soon after she'd found him was a crushing blow, and she was unable to reconcile the need for such a loss. How could a kind-hearted fellow be caught-up and devoured by a war fought between families just like her own? Her grief, as real as it was, couldn't last but was it swallowed up by the insurmountable anxiety and misery that loomed over everyone? Anguish, itself, seemed to rain down from brooding clouds and, subsequently, rise like a heavy strangling fog. All one's senses were out of balance. The world was out of balance.

Kate shook her head gently to dislodge her heavy ruminating and marveled for just a moment at her new-found confidence. She didn't know where it had come from; maybe it was just that there was little to lose anymore. The feeling of freedom and possibility felt good. She'd endured a lot; she could survive what came next.

She reminisced. The place she'd come from in central Mississippi was dense with greenness but much drier than this southern region. Somewhere along the way, throughout the summer, it would become dusty for at least one, maybe more, extended period—three or four weeks maybe. The polite conversation about the weather would become worried contemplation focusing on the condition of crops and livestock and when the next rain might come. Some summers the corn, tobacco, peas, and even the grass would go brittle. These were tough years when food became scarce for families, as well as livestock, and there began to be a ripple effect of the lack of rain on everything from Sunday supper to the national economy.

On many early evenings when she was a girl, she'd be distracted from her intended tasks by watching the gray squirrels chase each other through the trees, skittering over one extended limb and scaling across another, making fabulous leaps from one pencil-thin branch to another as they raced with unbelievable speed.

When she let her mind go, one thing did lead to another and another and another. She was thinking of the spring when she first noticed brown patches of leaves in the otherwise perfectly green-leafed pecan trees. She asked her uncle if he had a clue about what caused the decay, and he merely said, "tree rats." She went for days contemplating tree rats before she realized that he was talking about squirrels. She asked Old Man Possum about the tree rats, and he explained that in late winter when the food supply of the squirrel population diminished, squirrels chewed into the bark of trees to extract sugar which acts as a food supply substitute until their regular supply of pecans and other nuts, wild strawberries, muscadines, blackberries and such come in.

One morning in an unusually mild and moist early summer, she'd been fortunate enough to see a 'tree rat' walk pointedly up to a bright orange Chanterelles mushroom, snatch a portion of its trumpet-shaped cap off and munch on it right on the spot. Then, just a few moments later, again with lightning quickness, reach back and uproot the whole thing. She always felt privileged, like she'd been let in on a secret when she observed some minute or seemingly quirky act of nature.

After being preoccupied all morning with preparing the house that was too large for her alone for the winter, she walked down to the river bank and stood to reflect. Within seconds a blue heron took her breath away as it lifted its wings wide, directly out of the tree line along the river only a few feet of where she stood. She'd never seen it, but it was there within a few feet from her, stark white in contrast to the inimitable lush green surroundings. It was like the answer to the question that we turn over and over in our minds, searching for details, searching for direction and then the perfect epiphany presents itself to us right where we stand. She held the answer close to give herself time to be sure that this answer was the answer indeed.

Winter 1866

The winter had not been harsh, but it felt like it had rained
constantly since the new year. The quiet was beginning to be
maddening, even for Kate. She found herself carrying on a one-
sided dialogue with the day's rain.

Ah, here you are again.

We have quarreled and been at odds,

Each suffered at the harshness of the other.

If you're going to keep coming here every day in January,

we must call a truce and learn to embrace each other.

Yes, I anticipate the gifts that you will scatter across the yard and in
the fields beyond,

white narcissus and yellow daffodils growing in the soggy brown
embankment.

Yes, I'll take long winter naps with you,

giving up all that I have planned.

I'll do this for you because you ask, and now after all the resistance,

Letting go does seem to be the better option.

Yes, I'll drink warm jasmine tea with you and consider

All the good stories that we could write together.

Yes, I'll sit with you, feet propped up, bundled in the softest quilt

and read my favorite passages aloud.

Yes, I'll move the potted plants I tend for sentimental reasons back

and forth from the spots where they are safe from frost to the
a place where you can embrace them and sustain their greenness.

Yes, I'll submit to you and accept the gifts that you so consistently
bring in this
otherwise stark winter.
Let me tie on my boots, and I'll meet you on the wide porch.
You, gentle winter rain,
I know you, too, are waiting for the sweet explosion of spring.

She thought how crazy she'd sound to anyone else in the
house, should they hear her, should they be there, but they weren't.
She turned slowly and canvassed the front room. The house was too
big.

After breakfast Kate wandered the property, stopping here and
there to examine any natural phenomenon that caught her attention.
She'd been told by her dear friend Notch that she looked lost as she
walked among the gardens and orchards. She supposed she was
lost, lost in her thoughts. The seven camellia trees that had spattered
the world with a profusion of layered pink blooms at Christmas and
lasted even through the frozen days had all but disappeared now.
Except for the red-berried holly nestled in its glossy green, spiny
leaves, and camellias, she lamented the dreary time of year from
December into March.

The natural world was dormant; she'd even say withdrawn,
cloaked only in a thousand shades of browns and grays. The only
encouraging attribute that she could find in these bleak months was
her view into the woods, which was extended, allowing her to see
deeper into the forest than at any other time of the year. The quiet in
the winter woods was unlike any other time of the year. When she
took brief walks, she had trouble convincing herself that the rustling
of the crisp leaves, which had startled her, was a tiny titmouse rather
than some fearsome attacker. She laughed at her cowardice. And
then, of course, there were the hawks. She enjoyed watching their
soaring and circling. She'd noticed how they seemed to be
disciplined creatures of habit, settling every morning and every
afternoon on the same tree limbs, watching with perfect raptor eyes

for the field mouse or small snake that might present itself as the next meal.

She always enjoyed a ramble down to the little spring. In earlier years, a wooden box-like structure had been built directly on top of the small spring that bubbled up behind the dog-trot. The box had been lined with rocks gathered from across the property and near the river. The fresh water that filled the basin was cool and clear, sweet and delicious. The overflow from the spring created a small creek that trickled down to the Escatawpa River. The water at the farmhouse was supplied primarily through the cistern system with a hand pump or was pulled directly from the well using a bucket on a pulley. The spring water was a special treat.

On this morning as she wandered, she pulled her shawl tighter to comfort her from the slight chill in the February air. She halted immediately when her eyes locked on the small, soft, white trumpet throats along the hedgerow, and her face lit up as if she'd run into an old friend. Dozens of clumps of Narcissus danced in the wind. This was the first real sign that spring was pushing through the winter. She broke off a few stems of the pungent flowers to bring back to the cabin.

Kate had moved her essentials from the bigger farmhouse to the dog-trot where her husband's parents had lived as they built their larger home. The small weathered-wood cabin was built with one room on each side of the open hallway to allow for air circulation in the hot months and to further separate the wood stove and cooking area from the living area. It wasn't as well fortified from the elements as the farmhouse, but as the winter set in, Kate felt it was easier to manage and cozier. It met her needs. Kate had decided when she saw pecan trees put out their cylindrical, fuzzy caterpillar-like blooms, which her father had called tags, she'd plant sunflowers once again.

In the first summer at the Thompson's she marveled at the wide radiant faces of the deep yellow blooms. She'd wake early and walk through the dew-drenched rows of broad golden petals that towered above her. They must have been at least eight, maybe 10 feet tall, their velvety olive-shaded leaves bristling against her bare arms and dampening her loose morning dress as she stretched to cut a stalk here and there. She loved gathering fresh flowers and arranging them for the breakfast table before anyone else was stirring in the house. This memory of feeling alive in the sunflower patch exhilarated and inspired her.

Yes! She would again have a tall garden of these gems that would raise their faces and follow the bright sun as it slid across the summer sky. She'd rummage around in the storage spaces to see if she could find seeds salvaged over the years. Surely the seeds of them were still viable. As Kate's fundamental nature was hopeful, it didn't take much to revive that hopefulness when it dipped. The Narcissus, the possibility of sunflower seeds, as well as a faint whiff of Sweet Olive lifted her spirits immensely.

As she searched for the seeds, the big question of "What next?" became paramount. She'd find the seeds. She'd plant them as her farewell. She had no close relationship ties to hinder her. She could be adventurous, as adventurous as she'd ever dreamed—she would have to remind herself of this point. She'd go. She'd go to Brazil. She'd determine how to make the voyage possible—beginning this instant—and go. There weren't a lot of people to tell about her decision, but the first one would be Notch.

Kate spent the rest of the afternoon shaking debris from the gourds that hung along the eaves of the battered barn. Purple Martin scouts would be flying through soon, looking for new nesting places for their flocks. She wanted to be sure the farm was appealing enough for colonization in the spring, as these high-flyers were significant in helping to control the mosquito population, as well as other pests.

Once again, her best friend Notch crossed her mind as she remembered the day he brought the bundled gourds to the farm, during her second spring there. Notch had listened patiently as Jake ranted about State's Rights and Secession and how he'd surely join forces to defend Mississippi against any aggressor, even the United States government.

When Jake finished, Notch was quiet for a moment, then placed his hand lightly on Jake's shoulder and said, "People who will profit from such a war are stirring the pot, dear friend. At the core, the answer is simple. Slavery is wrong for any human being. Don't allow the topic to be diverted and watered down by other concerns, real or imagined. I say put your enthusiasm into devising an agrarian economy that does not rely on slave labor."

Kate re-hung the last of the gourds, picked up her tools, and headed to the cabin. The color was fading from the day as night was beginning to fall, even as the full moon, a blue moon, was rising quickly. Kate shuddered as she remembered it was also the night the newspapers had predicted a total eclipse of the moon. Typically, she didn't mind being alone, but she would've preferred company for this astrological event. As she was closing the door, she heard a bell ring in the distance and thought how clear it sounded. A bell in the winter, or, in this case, a cool early spring evening was different from the sound any other time of year. She supposed it was the quality of the air.

Last Days of April 1866: Departure

Kate could feel her heart beating strongly in her chest, as she slipped on her loose cotton dress and heard the first bird of a bright April morning sing. She loved hearing the morning sentinel of the mockingbird and chided herself on the days when her head was too cluttered and removed from the present moment to notice such a grand announcement of a new day.

When she stepped off the bottom back step into the dampness of the morning dew, she saw a most remarkable thing. Kate expected to wake this morning to bright sunshine, but instead heavy droplets of dew fell through the tree line like a warm sprinkling of summer. She found a morning wrapped in a blanket of fog made yellow from the pollen of every green thing trying to bud. As she slept straight through the night, a band of spiders wove a cocoon around her yard. Soft white filament, like single strands of cotton candy, stretched from the eaves of her porch across to the roofline of the old smokehouse, then from a deep-pink camellia bush to the weathered fence post on one side, camellia to lavender-shaded crepe myrtle on the other side. The result of the arachnid intensely weaving under the shine of the moon, along with the soft explosion of white-throated blue morning glories that trailed down the weathered fences on either side, made a happy surprise for the morning. She was amazed by this quiet transformation from the night. It felt like a gift for her departure to Baltimore.

Southwest Alabama; Late Winter/ Early Spring, 1866

"What is it that requires us to start over? What is it that allows us to keep pushing ourselves to accomplish a thing in the face of insurmountable odds? What is this loud voice that repeats over and over to us — 'persevere, stand your ground, persevere?'"

As he stood near the edge of the hard-packed clay street, he was still in earshot of the smoky conversation going on inside the front room, and he heard men's voices growl, "We're not a country of quitters! By God's grace, we'll find a way to rise from this gray, ashen soot. We cannot be destroyed. We'll bring our country back!" The graveled voice was full of the vibrato of H.D. Smith, always digging his heels in on one side or the other of a debate.

Smith's declaration was followed by the emphatic, but flat comments of Andrew Sikes, "We must consider our options. We have been reduced to nothing here. Our resources, all of them — our finances, our fields, our system of government — all annihilated. I'm headed west. The air is thin there, good for thinking; I know that from my time at Picchu Pass." He repeated himself in a tone that indicated he might already be gone, "The air is thin there, good for thinking, good for what comes next. My decision is made."

John Foster watched swaths of dark clouds slide across the face of the full moon like veils of Turkish dancers. The thunder that had rumbled in the distance now slammed like a heavy door blown shut, loud enough to startle him from his ruminating about the disturbing images of the past four or five years that had surfaced this evening — images of battles, burnings, destruction, starvation as fresh as an open wound had risen to the surface of his thoughts, like the back of a Mississippi mud turtle at the water's edge. Another loud crack; and a light rain began to fall. John Bailey looked at the moon again, felt the first drops of the easy rain on his face, pulled his hat lower, turned, and walked directly with intention, towards the garbled conversation.

He took off his damp hat and hung it on the mirrored walnut hall tree just inside the door. Catching a glimpse of his reflection, he could see for himself the telltale signs in his face, the resolute line of his jaw an indicator that his course of action was non-negotiable. He was a man prone to saying what was on his mind, no matter the situation, no matter the moment, but this time for some inexplicable reason, he circled the edge of the room as if walking the path around his cow barn, almost oblivious to the barrage of words being thrown back and forth.

He watched closely the faces of the men who were intense and exhausted in their continual calculation of exactly how to proceed in carrying on with their lives. He stopped, took a deep breath and projected his thoughts above the low rumble of the crowd, "I'm going to make my way to the Amazon. I'm going to see for myself what the Brazilian government is offering."

Several voices, indistinguishable in the crowd, blurted in unison, "What? You're going where? To do what?"

"I'm going. I'm going to the Amazon, to Brazil. My uncle was a Baptist missionary there when I was a young boy. I remember his stories about the fertile land and bountiful flowering trees; I've seen several notices in the *Alabama State Journal* posted by the Brazilians. I think it's time I took some action and checked into the so-called incentive. We won't know if it's an opportunity or not if we don't investigate it."

"John, you can't be serious. Have you lost your mind? We can't believe for a moment that you're serious about this!"

"I am. I'm certain and serious. I can't even tell you that I know why, but I am. We kick this red clay all day long every day, and we come up with nothing, but 'persevere, put our heads down, bow our backs and get through it.' The Brazilian government may be offering a viable alternative to the impossibilities that we lumbermen and cotton growers are facing here with the federals. Sikes may be on to something too, but oddly enough, I think that the South American jungle may be more kindred to our ways than the arid American West."

"John, what about your place, Cynthia, and your daughters? John, what about them?" asked old man Dan Taylor, an attorney who knew the personal business of almost everyone in the county.

"I've lost my only son to this ludicrous war whose aftermath is bound to destroy everything else." John Foster's voice waned and took a sentimental tone: "I hope that Cynthia will go with me. You men are the first to hear my declaration about this venture because I, just moments ago, settled my mind on it. I need to say this right here and now. My daughters both nurse wounded husbands. They have little to sustain them now. I'll call them back home, so they'll be together in this effort. I'll ask Cynthia to go with me. I don't know that she will, but I'll ask her to go so that she can see this place — Brazil — first hand."

As questions and cautions filled the air, his voice gathered strength, and he seemed to be talking to himself rather than anyone. "I'm going. It's time." His keen blue eyes were sharp in their decisiveness." If anyone wants to join me, come out to Yellow Pine. Be quick about it." John Bailey Foster walked directly out of the smoke-filled room, and inhaling the damp smell of pine, he lifted himself onto the broad back of his buttermilk buckskin quarter horse and slowly left the flickering lights of Creektown behind and headed into the woods he knew and loved so well.

"John! Have you lost your mind? You think you're going where? You think you're leaving me and going where? What uncivilized, heathen place do you mean to go exploring around like some young buck? John, you're not a young man anymore, and you're not leaving me here with everything there's to do to bring this place back to order. Do explain this to me, now!"

John's appearance was always neat and pulled together. Even though he had a reputation for speaking his mind, for the most part, his temperament was under control; this morning was no different. He wore the shirt that he'd pressed himself to save Cynthia from the additional heat put off by the heavy black cast iron, heated by setting it on the back of the wood-stove, while she prepared his breakfast of biscuits, over easy eggs and white hominy grits. She was frying bacon brought in from the smokehouse. Meat was scarce even for a family of their standing, or rather what had been their standing.

As he reached up to the top shelf of the cypress cabinet for cane syrup stored in the clear squat jar with a tarnished, dented tin lid, he noticed the drying skin of his hand and knew that she was right, he was getting old. This journey he had in mind was going to be arduous, but he felt that he was up to it. He had always been "up to" whatever task had presented itself. He had always taken pride in his physical strength, especially the strength of his legs. In his younger years, he'd joined up with any tracking or exploration adventure that came before him.

After he bought the farmland in the piney woods of southwest Alabama, he'd participated in all the work of establishing their home and timber business, from clearing and building to herding, planting, and harvesting. Before the war, his fierce intensity regarding everything with which he was involved was his trademark. The success of Yellow Pine Farm & Timber was an example of his optimism and enthusiasm, as well as his skill. The farm had been a dream realized, but it had become faded and worn, as if the house and everything around it was a sepia representation of itself, like an old worn photograph.

In a way, he felt there was no choice about the finality of the decision he'd made to head to South America. Even though the decision had come to him quickly, there'd been no other ideas competing for their future; none that seemed viable to him anyway. He knew now as he'd always known, he had to watch his wording with his wife. It was true he could typically keep his anger in check, but Cynthia's temperament was a different story. She'd always allowed her emotions to turn on a dime and this morning was no exception, not that he'd expected it to be. He allowed himself to think back for a moment to the second year of their marriage when he regularly caught her by surprise, easing up behind her, scooping her tall, almost willowy frame, into his arms and lifting her feet just off the floor. Her perfect, single walnut-colored braid flecked with auburn and golden highlights hung down the center of her back. Cynthia's wide brown eyes, even then, could go from soft doe-like orbs to sharp, chastising darts without warning.

He remembered her as she'd stood near the window that spring morning just over 20 years ago. The profile of her body showed her rounding belly through a loose white cotton gown as she stood barefoot, looking at him from across the room with some look of resolution that he still didn't understand, "John Bailey, your baby has begun to move." She'd finally smiled at him, and he moved in a straight line directly to her, overcome with joy and a real sense of being blessed.

He shook his head slightly to help dislodge the memory, "Cynthia, look at me. Look at me now," his voice nearly demanded. "I've said nothing about leaving you. This sojourn is not about leaving you. This trip, exploration if you will—I know it's iffy, but we have few other choices, and I believe this one to be the best for us. How can I provide for us when the means to do so is all but nonexistent? You're right, Cynthia. I'm not a young man anymore, and it'll take years to build our lives back here if it's even possible. I know it may very well be an unpleasant journey and will present difficulties, but I want you to come along. I want you to see this place with me. Come see for yourself what it might be like to live there."

Cynthia's brown eyes narrowed. Her hair was tied loosely back from her face, as she prepared their meal. She checked her emotions but met John dead-on. "I'm not leaving here to soothe your case of Brazil Fever, John. I'm not. And, if you do, you're leaving me as well as your home. I've had it with your lack of concern for me. You can call it what you will, but you can't face another day here. You have always wanted to wander. Now, you think you have your chance. I'll send for Mary Beth and Alice Jane to come home. I'll do what I can do to help them, and they'll help me—without you."

"Why, why, why do you have to be so close-minded and stubborn? I want to do my best by you Cynthia and by our family, and I believe with every ounce of my conviction that this is the best thing to do, and now is the best time to do it. These are unusual times, and they do call for extraordinary measures. It's not like I'm off on some lark. Earlier this year the *New Orleans Delta* newspaper had an article about General Woods who is the chief agent of associations of immigrants for several counties in Mississippi, and his experiences last summer in Brazil and with the Brazilian government. He has set forth several requirements on behalf of Southerners relocating to that country including freedom of worship and immediate citizenship. It's not like I thought this idea up on my own, but what if I did? There's been numerous correspondence addressing the possibilities and options. The article said the general had received them most enthusiastically."

Cynthia's sarcastically sharp come-back was only, "Big city news!"

Cynthia's comebacks were always sharp. Although John had a quick temper, a trait characteristic of his dark rusty hair, he seldom lost it with her. Even now as she'd battled him all morning, he sat in the ladder-back chair, leaning against the kitchen wall, with his heels hooked over the bottom rung and a slight tension in his shoulder that perhaps only she could detect because she'd known him most of his life. His hands were open and lay flat on the thick wide-planked pine table as he enumerated his plan.

"From the best that I can figure, from what I've been told and what I've read, the most expedient route to South America is actually out of Baltimore and would take about a month's time. I've researched it. After the ship's departure, the trip should take just about 40 days. I anticipate spending two months scouting the area; then, will return in nearly the same amount of time. Cynthia, I want you to come with me, but if you won't, I still must do this. I know in my heart it's the right thing. I'll go as soon as I can and be back the same."

Cynthia, losing all composure, screamed as she went down the back steps, "This is the work of the devil, John!"

He watched her, and his heart ached for her as she hurried past the pomegranate trees into the edge of the pecan grove where she slowed and began to pace. He understood her desire to keep everything the same, but he also knew that little would ever be the same. She'd always been one for maintaining the status quo, whatever it was at the time. He'd always been the one to push to expand the farm or dabble in business, as he felt was his responsibility. Cynthia had always made it harder than necessary. He knew this idea was just beyond her comprehension. He watched, and he loved her for all they'd endured together—the birth of three children, the loss of a son, risky wagers to build the timber business, a short stint in state politics—there by his side she was—fuming, but there.

Late the next afternoon, John questioned his Blue Tick Coonhound, Jack, that had rambled by his side through the woods and down to the Dog River and back. "It was a good catch today, wasn't it boy?" John pried a sizable rusty nail from the split rail fence post causing a puff of dust to rise, dug around in a canvas bag of miscellaneous brackets, nails, and various ties to find just the right size replacement nail.

Mindlessly, he whistled a low tune, reached in a larger, thick wet canvas bag and drew out a good-sized catfish, probably about three, maybe four, pounds. He grabbed the fish by its gills being careful not to get whipped by the whiskers of the fish. Using the blunt side of a hatchet for three hard raps, he pegged the nail between the catfish's eyes into the fence post near where he'd removed the old one. He pulled out his pocket knife with the thin, worn blade that made perfect work of the skinning. With the sharp tip of the knife, he circled the fish's body just below its gills, cutting only to the flesh in the circumference, still avoiding the spine.

John knew from a lifetime of experience that an encounter with a catfish spine was a painful thing to endure. He separated the skin of the fish from the flesh, making it easy to grab hold of the skin and pull downward, leaving only the light pink tinted flesh. With the sharp pocket knife, he gutted and filleted the fish in preparation for the family's supper. As John skinned fish after fish, he began to watch the early evening sun play off the gray skin reflecting it as if it were a shiny new galvanized bucket, then, deepening and dulling the color until it was more akin to flat pewter. This transmuting impact of light on color wasn't lost on John. He fully appreciated the play of light at any moment of the day.

John gathered the remains of the fish in a bucket and took them to the edge of the woods to bury them, a method of disposal he employed to try to keep wildlife at bay that might be seeking the heads and entrails. He didn't want to encourage any unwanted wildlife to come near the house. And, he certainly didn't want to hear a panther scream tonight, which it would do if it found the fish remains.

John's mind quickly moved to the hoecake and turnips that would accompany their dinner. He turned, walked to the well, and lowered the bucket, his mind blank, somehow quiet now. His breathing was steady as he slowly wound the crank that raised the wooden bucket of cool water dangling from a thick rope. Just as a last ray of sun glinted off the side of the tin dipper, he thought of the first time he'd met Cynthia; her mouth turned down just a bit at the corners, which seemed to make her smile more of an effort than it should have been. He had fallen for her instantly. And, while he did truly love her, their marriage had turned out to be far different from what he imagined on that first autumn afternoon. He kicked his boots gently against the side of the well to scrape the mud from the river bank loose.

Out West

Even though Andrew Sikes was 15 or 20 years younger than John Foster, they'd been good friends for a long time. Drew was only aware of one time in which there had been tension between the two of them. Drew supposed he may have been out of line to show interest in John's oldest daughter, Mary Beth, just as she was becoming engaged to the Smith fellow. John believed Mary Beth had made a clear decision and wise decision that did, in fact, include his fatherly input and he didn't want anyone, not even Drew, interfering in the chain of events that were in place to ensure his first daughter's chance for a secure financial future and would enhance her opportunity for happiness.

Drew knew that John Foster was highly protective of his family, maybe sometimes to their detriment, but that was none of Drew's business. John could run his family the way he saw fit. Drew knew too, that even though John was a friend he could trust with his life, John would never trust Drew with his daughter's life; he wasn't stable enough, nor traditional enough in John's eyes, for his daughter's future. Drew knew John had strong, clear feelings about the kind of life he wanted for his daughters; but, there was enough of the right kind of tension for the two men to form a sound business partnership and friendship.

John walked into the little cafe as Drew was mulling over the past six or seven years. John ordered them both a coffee and dragged a chair nearer Drew. "What you got on your mind, big boy?"

"John, I've just been sitting here thinking about that battle out west, north of Tucson at Picacho Pass. What a crazy time that was. You know, John, it wasn't a big scrap, but when a man loses his life, it's a monumental battle for him. There wasn't but about two dozen troops in The Pass both sides considered. There was a handful more of them than us. It was a beautiful day in April, the 16th, I think it was. Yellow poppies spread like a blanket waving across the pass.

Some things didn't make a lot of sense to me, just like those poppies in the desert, but the locals said they'd had a good rain that spring which made it so. We'd gone up to Picacho from Tucson where we'd seen fig, olive, and pomegranate growing, and even some fine fields of tobacco. Can you imagine that John? In the desert? It just goes to show sometimes we don't know all we think we know about a thing, which reminds me of a story you'll like, John."

"Let me hear it."

"Well, as the battle went, we took a position in a line of mesquite trees."

"Mesquite?"

"It's a tree with a thin leaf and a thick black bark. We don't have them here, but mesquites and the cottonwoods are what you see in the West. The mesquites gave good cover, and the Union's man Barret led about 13 of their guys in one at a time, single file. After less than two hours of nasty engagement, the sweet smell of mesquite was replaced with the heavy smell of gunpowder. They lost a lieutenant and a private, and I believe another ole' boy died later from wounds. They took Sergeant Holmes, Dwyer, and Hill as prisoners that day. I hated to know that, but I figured at least they were alive. It seems the Yanks were looking for a Captain McCleve who was supposed to be an asset to them. We had him, and they didn't get him back."

"You had McCleve, Drew? How'd you get him?"

"John, it was hard to tell who was military and who wasn't, particularly in the Confederacy, you know that, but especially out West. Some of those boys had never even seen a uniform, and while all that can be a disadvantage when you're trying to build a fighting unit, it can sometimes be used to your advantage too."

"You'll like this story, John. In March before this battle, I went with Captain Hunter and a handful of other troops to a place called White's Mill. Captain Hunter had a hunch that Captain McCleve from the Union side would be showing up there, and we needed information from McCleve. When we got there, we found that the trading post and mill owner, White, had been supplying the Union forces darn well. We were dressed in the only garb we had, which was a hodgepodge of styles. I mean, we surely didn't alert anyone by looking like a military fighting outfit. Most of us were carrying hunting rifles and Bowie Knives. We were wearing flat top civilian hats. One fellow, Fred, lost his first horse in a fight with some Mexicans but came out with a sombrero, which he wore every day and bragged about the good shade he carried with him. Now, that's a wide-brimmed hat, John, wide. I know you've seen drawings of Mexicans wearing sombreros. I, myself, was sporting a jacket from the Scottish Highlands. The point is, we caught White off guard; with little effort took him prisoner and held tight.

Sure enough, in a couple of days, McCleve shows up looking for some spy who seems to have gone astray. When he gets there, Captain Hunter is pretending to be White and gets all the information he needs from McCleve; then takes McCleve prisoner. Captain Hunter ordered us to confiscate all the clothing and arms for our men and gave a storehouse of wheat back to the Pima Indians, who grew it in the first place. There wasn't anything we could do with all that wheat. The Pimas were a pretty peaceful bunch — stayed fairly neutral throughout the whole thing."

"Hell, John, at Dragoon Pass Mail Station you had Unions and Confederates fighting side by side to hold off the Apache. Now, how mixed up is that?"

Drew continued, "But, get a load of this, In the 50's the U.S. and the Apaches had contracts, and the Apache were happy to have the easterners as allies against the Mexicans. Even the infamous Cochise had a contract."

"What goes wrong John? What goes wrong? Why are we always picking sides? You know, things aren't always what they seem."

"You've been doing a lot of thinking, my friend!"

"Yeah, I guess I have; and, I think nothing ever changes and nothing stays the same. I'm thinking about heading there — to Arizona. Arizona has been part of the New Mexico Territory, it's been a Confederate state, and it's a U.S. territory. It's a place that's accustomed to change. Maybe I can handle it better; maybe there's an easier shift in the world there. I don't know what kind of hunting they have, but I know they've got wild boars they call javelina, big bristle back things, Jackrabbits with tall ears and quail, pretty little things called a Gambel's quail. It prances around with a teardrop-shaped topknot on its brow. Of course, there's some nasty horned lizards and hairy scorpions. I've seen spiders big enough to make a man step out the way, but it's a place that sort of gets to you, John. By its immediate appearance, it ain't much, but there's an inexplicable tug. It's a rough country that's filled with risk, but paradoxically, there's a quietness there that evokes a strange kind of peace I've never known anywhere else. Some of the Indians call it the presence of the spirit world."

"Well, I don't know, Drew. It doesn't sound like my kind of place. I'm not sure I'd do well in the desert and be careful with all that Indian stuff."

THE VOYAGE

John Boards the Boat

John adjusted the heavy canvas duffle that he was carrying over his left shoulder as he stepped onto the gangplank of the *Isabella*. He was still trying to shake Cynthia's most recent tantrum and the subsequent silence of a tomb she extended as a parting gift when he left Yellow Pine a little over a week ago. John wasn't, however, shaken in his conviction that exploring Brazil was the most viable option for his family and the best choice. He never second-guessed the decision.

Check-in and boarding were required by Captain Briggs that evening, even though the boat didn't launch until late morning the following day. John was there early to be sure that everything was set for the trip and to get settled into his room, space which he came to refer to as CQ for cramped quarters. He liked having plenty of time to acclimate himself to what happened next, so he went straight to his personal area while the cargo was still being loaded, much of which included barrels of fresh water for the voyage. He felt right at home with the activity. He liked plenty of activity, always had—people moving about, shifting here and there—plans implemented, a sense of accomplishment.

John had a genuine desire to know more about the details of the arrangements. He pondered the calculations regarding the stops along the way and the factors that had been used regarding the weight of all the cargo, and he wondered about the challenges of refueling along the way. In the thick of things, he was as curious about the management and running of the vessel as he was about his destination.

Precisely 12 hours later on a bright Sunday morning, the *Isabella* pulled into the bay at Hampton Roads, Virginia. As it had previously served as a military vessel, the *Isabella* was made entirely of iron, and the captain and crew had required additional effort adjusting the compass bearings.

From this docking, John could see, as he'd heard some of the men describe, Fort Monroe, the location where Jefferson Davis was being held and had been held for the last year since his capture in Irwinville almost a year to the day. Word had it that Mrs. Varina Davis, after repeated petitions, had finally been granted permission to visit her husband. She'd been held within Savannah, even though no formal charges or accusations had been made against her.

John joined a group of men who introduced themselves but barely missed a cadence in their conversation. They included Joseph Matthews, an attorney that John would come to have respect and appreciation for and Dan Hall, a cotton planter, both of whom John would come to spend significant amounts of time. It appeared that amid differences of opinions and confusion about the fate of Mr. Davis, *The London Times* now advocated for clemency, not so much because of sympathy for Davis, but for what their editors believed was the best thing for the American Union. The politics of the country continued to be strained, and one strategy after another became twisted and dissolved.

Joseph continued, "I read, much to my surprise, Chief Justice Salmon Chase, who has voiced strong opposition to slavery from the get-go, is now saying that to put Jeff on trial for treason would be tantamount to public condemnation of the North. As he interprets the Constitution of the United States, secession is not treason."

The group was silent, and Joseph Matthews continued, "What this means, gentlemen, is that if the United States government makes a move to try Jeff for treason, it has a genuine risk of having the Supreme Court declare that the government had waged war illegally."

"You don't say?" was all that John could think to say, followed by the question, "What about all this talk about getting a pardon for Davis?"

"I think Jeff's response to the pardon talk, from the scuttlebutt that I've heard, was somewhat of a surprise to powers that be. As I hear it, several prominent men were building a groundswell for a petition that would ask for Jefferson Davis to be pardoned, but Davis, himself, wants no part of it."

"Why in the world would he not want a pardon?"

"To JD, a pardon means an admission of guilt, and he is refusing the tactic. The trial is what he wants."

"It seems as though there are no easy answers."

At 7:00 the next morning, they set sail towards their first scheduled stop, which was the island of St. Thomas in the Caribbean. John watched the mountain ranges of Puerto Rico slide by and was impressed by the number of ships coming and going in the area, particularly as they neared St. Thomas. The harbor, which was formed by an extinct volcano, was protected on all sides by rolling green craggy mountains. Dozens of sailing ships teetered in the bays, and tall sails billowed across the harbor. Smaller row boats taxied 10 to 20 people at a time to shore. Red tiled roofs of shops and homes dotted the shoreline, making a perfect crescent bayside as if to imitate the shape of the new moon. The steamer *Isabella* sidled along piers of the Danish Coal Wharf and anchored there.

John was dismayed at the thought of screening Americans for disease before allowing them to disembark to the island. And even though he thought the idea preposterous, he was more than ready to get off the boat for a while and allowed his initial reaction to stay on the boat as a matter of principle to be overridden by his interest in giving his legs a real stretch by walking the perimeters of the dock at a fast pace. Besides, they were going to be docked for two full days, and he had the letter that he'd written Cynthia to mail. About two hours after the health officer conducted his review, the passengers were allowed to go ashore.

In a later conversation with the some of the deck hands, John learned that in the previous decade the island had been struck by yellow fever, which not only cost many lives but cost significant loss in revenues due to the quarantine by the Dutch who were in possession of the island. John's indignation was soothed a bit with his appreciation of the tragedy that had befallen the island in recent history.

As soon as the passengers disembarked, and Captain Briggs signed the necessary documents, a group of shiny faced Negro women headed towards the boats in a single line, most of them, oddly enough, wearing white dresses to their mid-calf and bound at the waist by coal-smeared aprons. On their heads, they wore bulky padded headdresses that extended the crowns of their heads. Men wearing white pants scooped coal chunks from huge platforms stacked two and three men high with hard black sooty chunks.

John was surprised by the sheer number of Negroes who worked the docks, their bodies sweating. They were as black and damp as the alluvial mud of the Mississippi Delta. Later, he learned that of the islands' entire population of 15,000 people, 12,000 were Black; mostly French Blacks.

The women walked as straight as bean poles towards the steamer, carrying baskets of coal on their heads that must have weighed 50 pounds or more. He remembered one of the conversations he'd had with Samuel Blithers down by the river when he'd described this very ability of the Africans to carry large loads on their heads. John was amazed at the process but still didn't understand why people—women—would carry laundry, coal or whatever, on their heads.

Even though Cynthia had disavowed John in every tirade she'd thrown in the weeks before his departure, John made a beeline for the dock exchange office and left a letter for her there. As he understood it, a reliable system of mail transfer had been established from St. Thomas via the steamer *New York*, which picked up mail bound for the United States on the 22 of each month, just a few days away. The timing was good.

John loved Cynthia out of a habit that was more than two decades long, and the letter was an act of his sense of obligation. He knew that Cynthia would be expecting it, and he didn't see any reason for him not to try to meet this expectation. However, he wasn't truly aware of its matter of fact tone and how little affection it conveyed. He listed the people he spent most of his time with on the boat—mostly businessmen, and potential land scouts. He referenced that there were women aboard and even though he knew it would inflame Cynthia further, he couldn't help saying that these women were of a wide age range and seemed to be making the journey with ease. He also referenced his daily Bible reading from Leviticus to let her know that he hadn't gone completely insane.

John was typically a man of action, physical action. He was accustomed to accomplishing tasks, walking a pace with a sense of direction and responsibility. He asked Chief Engineer Beard and the crew every question imaginable regarding the construction and steering of the steamer. There had been conversation after conversation with new traveling acquaintances Doc McCort from just across the state line in Mississippi, Dan Hall of Georgia, and Joseph Matthews from central Alabama. They talked about the specific steps that would be taken after they arrived in Rio de Janeiro. John liked to plan, make lists—anticipate the details of projects.

John read his Bible diligently and kept up with his journal amazingly well, even though he'd never considered himself much of a writer. He did feel it was essential to keep track of his journey as he wasn't sure which details might be important later. He was baffled at how easy it was to lose count of the days of the week. It was easy enough to calculate the time of day because he had the sun to guide him there, but with his tendency to seasickness and then to boredom, the days slid seamlessly into each other.

There had been trouble within two days of leaving St. Thomas. The *Isabella* had moved entirely out of sight of land and remained that way for 13 more days. In the first leg of the journey from Virginia to St. Thomas, he glimpsed land here and there, every day or so, as the steamer pushed through the Caribbean islands. Now, there was no land. As the steamer pushed into the wind, her deck was in near constant rocking motion caused by the outer wind bands of a tropical storm that was moving through the North Atlantic Ocean. John had difficulty adjusting to the movement and was overcome by queasiness for days. For the first time, he felt some question about his stubborn pursuit of South America. Tomas, the cook, missed John's hearty greetings at breakfast and guessed the problem. He sent the galley boy to John's cabin with a stout dose of magnesium, which, after several hours, did help calm John's internal workings.

John was relieved to have his sense of stability return, but his spirits remained dampened. Feeling restless, he'd begun to mumble to the gentlemen around the card table that the trip was proving to be monotonous with the same dull sea life day in and day out. Due to his occasional queasiness, John had taken another dose of magnesium before bedtime and felt much better the following day, but to be on the safe side, he avoided breakfast.

With just a little calculation he reassured himself that it was indeed Saturday, June 1st. John had always felt it was important to maintain a sense of decorum. Dressing appropriately was, in part, how he believed men maintained their status, which in his mind was indicative of their power, so he dressed in his better clothes, which may not have been trendy, but were undoubtedly respectable and classic.

He tied the ribbon in a horizontal bow under the tall stiff collar of his white shirt. He was aware that the wide cravat wasn't the latest style, but given the circumstances, fashion was a great luxury that he couldn't afford. He buttoned his vest that was cut deep to show the white shirt and pulled on his frock coat, which struck him mid-thigh. He tucked his treasured pocket watch in and straightened his seam lines here and there. Then he combed his burnt copper hair straight back from his broad forehead and directly back over each ear. That's when he noticed a few fine gray hairs mingling on each side of his head. He hated that. The gray showed in his beard too, which he wore tight. "Could be reason enough to shave it," he said aloud to himself. Even John was surprised when his vanity showed up. He shrugged, then pulled the door closed and absently began whistling "She Waits by the River for Me."

John headed upstairs to the top deck and was genuinely grateful for the ocean breeze and calm water. He nodded to the ship's first officer, to Doc McCort, his friend Joe Matthews, and to other groups of men gathered here and there as he casually strolled the perimeters with his hands clasped behind his back.

Other than the card games with his new acquaintances and occasional lounges on the deck, John spent much of the 15 days between St. Thomas and the northeastern port of Brazil, stowed away with his Bible. He was both traditional and conservative in his religious beliefs, but he did hold out the possibility that God might indeed intervene in personal lives in unlikely, subtle, and profound ways. Maybe he was trying to see if his Uncle Bart, the missionary, would reveal himself. After all, he'd used Bartram Hayes' adventures as part of his defense for making this trip in the first place.

Notch and Kate

Kate Teal was born on a cold, bright December morning, just three short months after the Treaty of Dancing Rabbit Creek was signed. A long time passes before some of us can understand the full weight of the stars under which we're born. Single events which seem remote can have lasting implications as the universe into which we push, shifts; then nothing is the same.

Kate's father who had been a farmer and a legislative aide was present for the negotiations of the Treaty at Dancing Rabbit Creek in central Mississippi, and she'd grown up listening to stories of the Choctaw debates. It must have been a fantastic sight that September when seven elderly Choctaw women sat with 60 chiefs, other tribal leaders, thousands of villagers—mostly Choctaw—and a few Americans, as days of negotiations and intimidation led to the signing of the treaty which was the last step in setting in motion what would become known as the Trail of Tears.

The women were against selling their country. They were against moving to the western frontier, and they were against the requirement of becoming citizens of the United States, if they stayed in Mississippi, even if the government promised them land for their allegiance. They felt it was a foolish mockery. People couldn't own land any more than families could be forced to leave the spirits of their ancestors.

None of it made sense, but the conversations grew more and more divergent and intense, scare tactics increased until on September 27, 1830, the treaty, the first premise of which was perpetual peace and friendship, was signed. All Choctaw who remained at Dancing Rabbit Creek beyond the two-year transition period would be required to become United States citizens, consequently making the Mississippi Choctaw the first major non-European ethnic group to gain citizenship in the United States. A third of the Choctaw stayed, and the rest left for what they believed to be their freedom and the right to make their laws. Those who remained to maintain as much normalcy as possible in their ancient land had, for the most part, become sharecroppers by the time Kate had grown into adulthood. Of course, at this point, Kate was still asleep to the tumult that would challenge her to be startled awake in her own life. She hadn't even seen it coming. No one could've.

Now, just over three decades later, another debate about choosing homelands, albeit vastly different ones, had become complex and insufferable.

Kate & Notch Board the Boat

Kate and Notch arrived at the docks late in the afternoon about an hour before the final call for passengers. They were very comfortable together, always had been. It wasn't immediately noticeable that Notch was Choctaw. His complexion was only a shade or two darker, a smooth olive tone—a reflection of his French ancestry. His eyes were as dark as the sea at night and his hair, fashionably cut, was crow black making him stand out among a group of mostly fair Scottish, English, and German descendants. Kate was excited but amazingly relaxed at the same time. Her breathing was deep and even.

In her excitement, she would point here and there making sure Notch was seeing everything that she was seeing. Once Kate made her mind up, she became committed to her decisions. She felt very good about this trip and believed that what came next, whatever it was, would show her a clearer path to the choices she'd need to make for the future. Even though she was a dreamer, she looked only short distances ahead. Life was full of variables and contemplation of too many of them clouded her ability to act. Notch and Kate moved through the port and up the platform looking like an unremarkable couple.

They were similar enough in age, although he was a few years younger, and the two were casual enough in the way that they related to each other for people to presume they were a married couple. They spent hours talking, and sometimes Notch would take both Kate's hands and rest them in his as he spoke to her. It had become their daily practice to watch the sun slip into the vast expanse of ocean, but most days at sunset they didn't talk at all.

Kate spent most of the day every day on the main deck of the boat. She'd brought plenty of books for them to read. Notch sat next to her whether he read or not. Inevitably, they moved from one side to the other as the sun and shadows shifted. Eventually, at some point each day, she'd say, "Let's walk, Notch."

"*Itanowet ia*" (yes, let's walk together).

Kate wore a broad-brimmed hat tied just under her chin with a wide dark blue ribbon. The hat was more to shield her from the sun than for a fashion statement. As she walked, she was forever tugging at the light shawl, a shower of tightly woven purple pansies that slid around her shoulders.

Notch didn't need a lot from other people, never had. He had come along on the trip to accompany Kate, ensure a certain level of safety, maybe even propriety that oddly enough he felt responsible for providing, although responsibility was a strong sentiment. He enjoyed Kate's company, always had, and was just as happy to be with her now as to be anywhere else in the world. Notch was genuinely capable of focusing on the present moment without even considering what he might do when he got to Brazil. Of course, he'd thought about it, but he hadn't tried to figure out the details. He knew Kate would be working on that part anyway—the details. He wasn't waiting for her to resolve his future but knew full well that one day soon she'd break forth with a list of "Maybe you could do this, Notch" kind of ideas.

Some days the two would walk without much conversation. Some days Kate was animated by one idea or another. She could be a bit intense in trying to make her thoughts understood to Notch because many times, she was still working them out as she spoke, anticipating that she was on the verge of some new understanding. But, mostly the talk had to do with what she was reading and what Notch might think of it. Henry David Thoreau was at the top of her list. His writings describing the relationship of nature to man had always intrigued her. She was reading, for the first time, a collection of essays called *Excursions*.

Kate felt she did her best thinking when she was walking The *Isabella* was a coal steamship; the upper deck open to the sea was long and wide providing plenty of space for her contemplation. A great white canvas tarp was tied across the width and length of a gathering area and hung low like a dense cloud. Its grand bellowing motion made her feel as though they were riding the fleshy translucent fins of a giant stingray. But, when she looked inward instead of out to sea, it was easy for her to forget she was in the middle of the North Atlantic Ocean.

Groups of men gathered about in clusters, as men will do, reading their international newspapers collected in St. Thomas. Many of them smoked pipes and cigars, expounding on happenings that were taking place around the world, including the fact that Alexander II, the Russian emperor who emancipated the serfs in 1861, had, just a few months prior, narrowly escaped an assassination attempt. The men also talked about the emperor's interest in selling the Alaska district to the United States.

The hardwood floors of the ship were maintained to a high standard. The outer cabin walls that encased the stairwell to the decks below were of polished mahogany veneer. Some of the women pushed chairs and side tables against the cabin wall to block the salty sea breeze as they read or worked their fingers with crewel needlework or knitting. Most found it best to be practical with their hairstyles as the winds made high maintenance of loose styles, so they pulled their braids high and pinned them back lengthwise to the center of their heads, minimizing the effect of the sea salt.

Kate's style was casual for her time, but even so, she conformed as much as she felt reasonable, to the protocol of the day. She was amazed each day that the young girls were outfitted in their best dresses and leggings as if they were attending an event or going someplace special, which upon consideration, Kate brought her thoughts full circle. How odd it was to be so finely dressed when they were confined to the ship day in and day out; yet, indeed they were going someplace special—the Future.

The children, of whom there were at least a dozen on the voyage, loved the upper deck too. Here they had long spaces for foot races, and the girls drew squares for hopscotch jumping. Children loved Notch. They were drawn to show him their spinning tops or how they could jump higher or further than anyone else. Occasionally, Notch would spot a rogue jack or a yellow cat-eye marble that had escaped from the bunch. He invariably would hold on to it until they came looking for him, "Mr. Notch, Mr. Notch have you seen my cat-eye?" And they all laughed aloud. Kate loved the children's jubilation when they spotted sea life near the boat; she shared their excitement.

In the first leg of the trip, the nine or so days to St. Thomas, Kate and Notch were equally awed by the intense shift of ocean blue and green color in the Caribbean. Notch was the first to remark how the island lifted from the sea like great turtle backs rising above the water line, surrounded by clear azure and turquoise waters. As the ship pressed closer to the shore, the lines of ports, buildings, palm trees, and huts became distinct. They both marveled at how often these turtle backs lifted from the water, became islands, and disappeared again. Hardly a day went by without land in sight, which would not be the case in the latter part of the trip.

When Notch confirmed that the large island to the east was Hispaniola, Kate remembered that Christopher Columbus had visited these islands. Notch teased and questioned whether Kate was like that long line of white men who sought to discover "the new world." He understood that his comment could've been construed as bitter, which it was with historical regard to the Europeans who exploited the world in which his ancestors had lived, but not towards Kate, who had always held a special place in his heart more than that of a sister, maybe as *haiyup atta* (twin).

As the *Isabella* slipped past Hispaniola, Notch explained that the area in the northeastern side of the island called Samaná was where hundreds upon hundreds of former slaves and Black Freemen had emigrated from the United States for many years. He further explained that U.S. government had once had eyes on the Samaná peninsula to establish a military base but ended up choosing Cuba instead. He wasn't sure about the status of that endeavor.

When the turtle back called Puerto Rico surfaced and lowered again, Notch and Kate got word that they were only a couple of hours out of St. Thomas. They readied themselves for disembarking and took seats on the main deck, hoping to be strategically placed at the front of the line for disembarkation and looking forward to exploring the harbor and the city. Notch was especially happy that his two feet would soon be on land again—being neither sailor nor pirate and only a freshwater fisherman, he preferred solid ground.

After medical clearance was given, Notch and Kate, arm in arm, were among the first ones off the boat. Kate was dazed by the cacophony of sounds in the harbor, especially the strange mix of languages. She found the movement in the port dizzying. Notch's lighthearted attitude and thrill with being on land trumped any hesitancy that Kate may have been feeling, as he led them through the streets. The two moved on to side streets and watched the buzzing activity of island country.

Eventually, they realized that they'd independently started to scout restaurants for an early dinner. They watched what they discerned to be "the locals" and chose their dinner based on the popularity of those who seemed to identify the best cuisine. They chose to dine at a pavilion lit by torches at the perimeters, and here and there in the center aisles, which were created by rows of primitive tables aligned with heavy wooden benches.

The atmosphere was jovial and lessened the awkwardness of the language barrier. They were immediately served fresh bananas and mangos. Notch peeled and sliced the mango to share with Kate. As the sticky juice ran across the soft sweet yellow meat of the fruit through his fingers, Kate laughed, "It's like eating a huge giant wild plum, a monster plum, not like the ones in the thickets back home."

"You're the funny one, Kate! I wouldn't be peeling a plum for you back in the piney woods. This travel is spoiling you, but you could stand some spoiling."

"Life has been tough on all of us in a myriad of ways."

"Yes, and I know your resist, but just because your story is not the bleakest doesn't mean that you should not be indulged in these little ways from time to time. Now, sit back and enjoy your mango!"

The remainder of their dinner, which they ordered by looking at the plates of other patrons as they were being moved through the pavilion on large trays, consisted of Johnny Cakes made with flour, rather than the cornmeal they were accustomed to and callaloo which was a stew consistency and similar in color to steamed turnip leaves. Notch and Kate were both surprised when they tasted the chili peppers in the stew. They also had steamed fish and a side dish of a concoction which appeared to be made of onions, garlic, and bell peppers, called *sofrito*.

Kate was pleased that Notch had consented to travel with her as her companion on this trip. She felt a little guilty that he had come along as her "protector" rather than someone who'd set his sights on a new life in Brazil, but she also knew he'd been honest when he wholeheartedly agreed to go. They had enjoyed each other's company since the days that they were children chasing tiny yellow butterflies in the watermelon patches, and Notch had always been looking for the next adventure. He was a delight to be with on St. Thomas island.

John and Kate's First Conversation

On the third day out from St. Thomas, Kate noticed a strange quality of water on the port side of the ship. When her eyes were able to focus better and distinguish shapes, she saw a transparent mass floating, then realized the jelly-like substance was made of dozens of parts. Excitedly, Kate rushed from person to person and from small group to small group of passengers. She was filled with bemusement as she tugged at a sleeve here and there, laughed aloud, and motioned for others along the deck, "Come see! Come see, what's in the sea!"

John looked up from his chess game to see what all the fuss was about and saw Kate walking fast, almost skipping from group to group. John had noticed this woman before. He'd seen her come aboard with her husband, or so he thought, in Baltimore. She was attractive enough to catch his eye, but what held his attention was some still unknown quality about her.

Late one afternoon he found himself watching her as she stood motionless for the longest time looking out across the ocean as if she were unable to turn her eyes away. What he noticed first was the way the breeze blew her chestnut hair across her face. Most women wore their hair pinned up or tied back in public; hers was uncommon in that she'd freed it so that the wind brushed it across her face and she pushed it back from her face with her left hand while continuing to talk with her right.

John and the Captain joined the gathering, and the Captain proclaimed, "Man-o-war!" There were dozens of them.

"Those critters have quite the sting to them, can be deadly," the Captain explained, taking on the role as the docent of the sea. "They're named after the armed Portuguese warships of the 15th and 16th centuries, which flew triangular sails. Look at how this angled part of their body floats at the surface of the water. See how it's tinged with a bit of a blue color. Sometimes the color shows pink and even purple. This is just a small part of the creature you see here. This son-of-a-bitch, excuse me, Mrs. Teal, has tentacles that average 30 feet long, but can extend downward over ninety feet beneath the sea. The sting of the whips is very painful. These creatures usually drift in large packs. Wouldn't surprise me if there are hundreds of them near 'bouts. They're meat eaters themselves, but the old loggerhead turtle is a rare predator of these demons."

Kate's constant readiness to ask questions added to the youthful quality about her that betrayed her actual age, not that she was inappropriate, more like eager. "Are these related to the jellyfish I've heard about on the Mississippi/Alabama coasts?"

The captain replied, "Maybe related, but not the same. These are drifters, moved by the wind and waves." And he was off, distracted by another conversation.

Kate watched until the steamer had moved on, leaving the conglomerate of Man-o-War in its wake. John returned to the deck, unintentionally startling Kate by coming near her. "Mrs. Teal?" She turned abruptly and laughed at her exaggerated reaction. "I'm sorry, she said, "my mind wanders, and I believe I was lost in the moment!"

"I just wanted to say that I enjoyed your exuberance over the Man-o-War, a bit earlier. It's a pleasure to see such a joyous reaction to sea creatures."

"Hmm," Kate pursed her lips, "Perhaps I was a bit childish, but I'm always thrilled by the surprises that nature brings us and our days on this boat have been painfully calm; thank goodness! I think we're all afraid to complain of the dullness in case we conjure up a hurricane. The probability of a great sea storm did cross my mind more than once before I made the final decision to board this boat."

John, a tall fellow, tilted his head as if to align himself a little better with her height. When he smiled, she noticed the one dimple in his left cheek. "No Ma'am, not childish, a delight, just like I said."

Kate found the lightness and assumed underlying authority that flowed through his southern accent when he spoke pleasing to her. By his voice, she recognized him as a neighbor, even though she hadn't met him before boarding the boat. She smiled and began again, "We take so much for granted, Mr. Foster. While I feel that I should contain myself a bit more at times, I do believe it's a gift to be amazed at everyday events. For example, as we left the islands a few days ago, I found a new appreciation for the poetry in learning to say the word 'bird.' A fair-haired, round-faced toddler dressed in a sea-foam green pinafore, was watching the common terns and brown pelicans that were trailing along behind us. Her dark-haired, handsome young father repeated the words 'bird,' 'boat,' 'water.'

"Watching the child, I thought of her concentrated effort in trying to replicate the word 'bird.' I began mouthing 'bird' slowly to myself and thinking about how the word must feel the first time it formed in the mouth of a child. Bird. I'd think that the 'r' would be hard to find and that the first sound might be more akin to 'bud.' It seems as though it would tickle a bit coming through — 'burd.' First, the lips pout, and as a little puff of air blows outward, the tongue makes a quick lick to the roof of the mouth, and the odd sound 'burd' comes out. The amusing little word 'burd' gets forever attached to the feathered thing that lifts up and down in wind currents. Funny, how written language works as well, letters running out of pens connecting one to the other, a myriad of shapes making words in various languages and spaces making thought. Isn't it interesting that it takes space to create thought?"

Kate took a deep breath, pleased with her story, but a little self-conscious that she was rambling so.

John looked directly into Kate's blue eyes and chuckled, "Really now. Is that a fact?"

Usually, Kate was comfortable with silence, but at this moment the silence between them felt awkward. She rushed the conversation forward with information to fill the space. "I find languages are so interesting, but I only know our language and a few words of Choctaw that Notch taught me. I intend to learn primary Portuguese once we get to Brazil. I find it interesting that different cultures describe the same objects or concepts in different ways. Maybe the cache of descriptive words is relative to the way different cultures think. For example, in Mississippi, there's one word for snow, and near the coast, we don't use it very much."

"What about sleet and hail?"

"Well sure, there's sleet and hail, but that's not snow. The point I'm getting at is that people who live near the Arctic Circle where snow is the predominant landscape have dozens of words for snow. There's a word, which I can't pronounce for new snowfall, one for fresh snow accumulated on the top of old snow, one for snow on the roof and on and on like that. More specifically, I wonder how much about one's culture is indicative in its language."

John mused, "Culture, huh? I'm not exactly sure what you mean, like religion?"

"Religion is certainly part of the culture, but it's not the only facet that makes a culture. I think one's culture is representative of its belief system, including religion, but not limited to it. Other aspects that might make up culture is how a particular group of people view nature, how they view work and leisure, the foods they eat, their fears, their feelings of inferiority or superiority."

John gave Kate a quizzical smile, excused himself, and returned to the group of men who were calling him to join in their latest game of cards.

The next evening on the deck, John approached Kate. "I find that I'd like to share an incident with you. Is that OK, Mrs. Teal?"

Kate smiled and said she'd appreciate a story, and that he was welcome to call her Kate, short for Lillian Kate.

John began to tell her the story of how he met Samuel Blithers. "It was last spring when the Green Trout were bedding on the Escatawpa River, mostly we call it the Dog River." He saw the surprised look on her face.

"You said the Escatawpa?"

"Yes, that's it; it's a funny name." He observed an expression of recognition cross her face like hot coffee running through the body on a cold day.

"Yes, it's a funny name," she said. "The original name of the river was Choctaw, '*Oestcatawpa,*' which means to trim cane. In earlier years when the Choctaw lived more freely, they'd make annual journeys to the river banks to cut cane for weaving perfect baskets, which were vital to their culture for storing various items and carrying all sorts of supplies. 10 or 12 years ago when the United States Post Office opened a drop off location in the little settlement near the river in Mississippi, the spelling was changed to *Escatawpa*. And I, too, live or lived along that river!"

"Well, you don't say? Is that a fact? I knew you were a good egg. I don't live directly on the Escatawpa, but my home place isn't too far from it. I'm in, or as you say, have been in the timber business in southwest Alabama. My sawmill is dang near the state line. By the way, got any idea why they call it 'The Dog?'"

"I do." She looked hesitant.

"Well, go ahead, tell me."

"I guess, I don't know why they call it 'The Dog,' but I know how that name came to be."

"That's good enough. Go ahead."

"It seems as though French colonists along the Mississippi coast referred to the river as *'Riviere Au Chien,'* which of course is translated to English as Dog River."

"Well, of course, it is." He laughed.

"Are you making fun of me, Mr. Foster?"

"No indeed, I'm impressed with you. How do you know so many facts about different, as you call them, cultures?"

"For much of my life, I've had plenty of time for reading. I do have a formal education. I married late. And, we have digressed. I'd love to hear about your sawmill, but you were going to tell me a story about a gentleman by the name of Samuel Blithers."

"Before the story, just curious, do you know anything about fishing?"

"I know the best time to catch crappie is when the dogwoods are blooming. My daddy taught me that when I was a little girl."

"That's good. That's good. Yeah, well Blithers is African. Me and him had both discovered a spot along the river where the fishing was good. You see, when the female Green Trout bed or lay their eggs, they'll find a sandy gravel river bottom near the bank and will scrub away a quarter inch or so with their tail, even to the point of making their tail bloody, in order to clear just the right spot to hatch the eggs. The female will rub her belly against an old cypress or pine stump or big rock that made her choose that area for her bed in the first place. When the soft eggs are deposited, she stays with the eggs for three to five days to protect them from other fish. The male fish then moves in and swims in circles around the bed, hovering over it, protecting the hatching process from intruders until the newly-hatched fish are about three-eighths of an inch long, when they leave the bed and swim off. With bait, a little skill, and some luck, you can aggravate the fish into striking, hook 'em, and end up with a nice mess of fish for supper."

"Three-eighths inch? That's not much supper!"

"Not the baby fish, the mama and the papa fish!"

They both laughed, and John continued, "For a couple of weeks Blithers and I had shown up along the same space at similar times. Every man knows that the best fishing is in the low light times of day, early morning or late in the afternoon. Anyway, we pretty much ignored each other. Neither of us willing to give up such a fine fishing spot just because the other was there."

The memory seemed to overcome John, and he was silent, thinking about his fishing companion back in Alabama. In addition to a great catch, he and Blithers appeared to find the peace that men see in fishing along a bend in the river. The act of fishing was practical with regard to what may or may not be on the supper table, but it was also an opportunity to remove oneself from the constant questioning of the moment, whatever it might be, and just exist in a place where there was no need for answers, no need for defense, no need for questions—just man and fish, a clear slow-flowing river, sunlight, a breeze from time to time and the occasional smugness of hooking a trout. John noticed the rhythm of his breath there and liked the feeling of peace that he found at the river. He knew Samuel Blithers would say the same thing.

It wasn't until John broke his last bit of fishing line on an old cypress sinker that any communication at all began between the two. John waded across the clear shallow river upstream a bit and then along the west bank side to the young Negro. "Sorry to bother you, but any chance you got an extra line in your bag there? I just snapped my last one on an old log."

"I might have somethin in 'ere that'll work." Blithers began to sort through his fishing pouch. Within a moment or two the man, whose hands were as dark as wet weathered wood, pulled out a line wrapped around a small flat rock that could've been an arrowhead. As John reached out his hand to take the line, he introduced himself, "Foster, John Foster, here." The man with the line returned, "Samuel, Samuel Blithers."

John offered the man a small trout from his fishing pouch in exchange for the line, before he distanced himself. He noticed right away that there was something different about Blithers, different from what he'd experienced with other Negroes—slave or freedmen alike, for that matter. He had thin scars on his face, thin, fine lines that might not have been noticeable had the sun not shone across his face exactly as it did. Blithers' eyes were as black as India ink. They were clear and strong, but it was their directness that surprised John the most. What had been said was enough for the moment; but, over the weeks, the two men came to nods as they appeared to each other here and there along the river's bank.

Men don't talk to each other, except in the unlikely event that they do. Maybe it was the sweet scent of spring along the river. Perhaps it was the angle of the sun. Perhaps it was an extraordinary time or the fact that two very different worlds had collided, undetected by the larger world, there on the Escatawpa at the same fishing hole, but the two men did begin to talk. John registered a feeling of superiority, but at the same time, there was unusualness about Blithers that allowed John to dispense, for the most part, with the conventional social structure that was second nature to him.

John found it difficult to admit, even to himself, that he'd grown weary of thinking day in and day out about what his next step would be. He'd always made decisions instantly, right on the spot; he'd been particularly decisive when it came to hard choices, but this time it was different. He'd gone back and forth in his mind for months trying to determine the best option for his family—dig in and start over, head out west, like Sikes, drop down into Mexico and wait it out, venture further out to the Amazon. What bizarre options they all seemed to be.

John sensed the African was in the same sort of mindset, and while each man had a guarded approach to the other, something in these moments on the river bank encouraged them to reveal much more than they would ordinarily. Ordinarily, they wouldn't have had a conversation, period; certainly not one of such a personal nature. Ordinarily, they wouldn't have fished side by side, but they weren't living in ordinary times.

John resumed his conversation with Kate. "The sound of the shallow rushing river over a slight ridge of rock here and there, an easy breeze in the yellow pine will bring what's on the heart to the surface. Perhaps I should have been more cautious, used more restraint in talking about my uncertainties. I'm sure Samuel Blithers thought the same, but that wasn't at all what happened. Maybe sometimes a story begs to be told. I told Blithers some of my stories, and he shared with me some of his—a remarkable story in fact."

"I guess Kate, until this conversation with Blithers, I'd never given a lot of thought to where slaves came from. I mean I'd certainly given thought to the institution of slavery and the commerce created around it, but not so much to the individuals themselves. Slavery was a thing, a commodity, a way of doing business that's been around for hundreds of years, not a person—a man, a woman, or a child. And yes, I've known Negroes all my life-—traded with some, had help with my mill from some, but the level of exchange was always about the work, never any personal connection. It was like rowing in separate boats that occasionally bumped into each other, then requiring interaction."

"Blithers said he wasn't American. Well, I never thought he was, but this is the way he explained it. Many of the slaves, I guess that's freedmen, do consider themselves American because not only were they born in the United States, but so were their parents and grandparents. The previous generations had been brought in along the eastern seaboard and bought and sold several times over, some ending up in the deep South—Mississippi, Alabama, and the like.

According to Blithers, these folks have lost their connections with Africa and know little to nothing but what they recognize here in the United States. Blithers said his arrival in the United States was different from that. Even though it had been illegal to bring internationally traded slaves into the United States since 1820, he'd arrived in the bay near Mobile after a six-week journey on the *Clotilde*, in the fall of 1859, just months before the war began. Blithers was in his mid-twenties at the time, making him about 30 when we met there on the river. As he told it, there were about 120 Africans on the boat, mostly young folks. He said that they came from several different places in Africa, I think he said seven different villages or regions and didn't even speak the same language. "

"Imagine that Kate, a boat full of people who look the same, but don't speak the same language. Have you ever thought of that?"

"Well John, a boat full of Europeans would look very similar, maybe even their dress, but some might speak French, some German, some Dutch and so on."

He was silent, looked at her without expression, then said, "You are right. What is it about the Africans that had caused me, and I dare say 'us' to think about them so differently?"

"I think you've probably already identified the cause, at least in part. Our culture has viewed slaves as a commodity. They were a collective of purchased lives, not individuals with hopes and dreams and profound love for their families."

"Blithers said they didn't even have the same religion. Well, if you can call it a religion. The only one he mentioned I'd even heard of before was Islam. Myself, I can't think much of any religion that isn't Christianity." He paused thoughtfully, "I guess in a way this speculation around religion speaks to your point, Kate. They were a religious lot whether it is a religion I recognize or not.

"Once Blithers started talking, I learned that some of the Africans on the boat were prisoners of war, the result of one African country fighting against the other, and some were kidnapped—that was especially applicable to the very young. Supposedly, and I guess I've no reason to doubt it. One of the captured was a nobleman in his country and a slave owner himself. Isn't that just a tangled mess?"

"There appears to have been some social mixing with the American free slaves, but get this Kate, there was skittishness about that too. It seems like these Africans from the *Clotilde* had a habit of standing straight and tall which was considered a bit uppity by some of the locals—Whites and Negroes alike. Samuel Blithers said that was because many of the Africans had been trained to carry heavy loads right on the top of their heads and that just naturally lent itself to a better posture."

"You know I witnessed Negro women in St. Thomas carrying baskets on their heads and sure enough they stood straight as a fence post. He said the folks where he was from in a mountainous area in northwest Benin, bordering the Gulf of Guinea and east of the bigger country of Nigeria, had lots of scarifications on their faces and bodies that looked peculiar to an outsider. But in their own countries, these scars marked rites of passage for the men, as well as the women. It's odd enough to me to scar up one another, but they also filed selected teeth to sharp points. These were just some of the obvious things that made Blithers and his neighbors different from the rest. It sounds right odd now, me telling you, but I've got to say again when Blithers told it, it just sounded like 'this is just the way life was.'"

"Blithers said a year ago when he and some other Africans were set to go up the Tombigbee towards Montgomery to support the Union Troops. Isn't that a shame Kate, 'to support the Union troops'? I got to tell you. I almost lost it with that African when he said that. But anyway, Blithers was relating his experience of it all. He said there was a lot of commotion going on and his crew spotted some Yankee soldiers eating mulberries. They went over and asked about the racket, to which the Union boys told 'um to leave, that they were free. When one of the African boys asked, 'Where do we go from here?' They just said, 'Wherever you want.' Blithers said that while the idea of finally being free again sounded good for all the Africans who had been enslaved for nearly six years, he immediately realized that a new kind of chaos was about to begin.

"Blithers had shaken his head and said, 'We were homeless; we didn't have any place to go.'"

"'We were house slaves and field slaves and even soldier slaves to a degree.'"

"Lots of folks want to get back to Africa, but some of them can't even really make it known where they're from because White maps aren't the same as our African knowledge of landscapes. Some Africans, like those on the *Clotilde,* were so young when they were captured that like the multi-generational Negro Americans, know only stories of their ancestors, but they don't understand where their homeland was."

"Blithers spoke about the fact that something called the American Colonization Society had paid for the passage of freed slaves to return to Africa but seems by the time word reached south Alabama and Mississippi all that money was gone. They'd tried hard to figure out some way to get passage fees, but wages, of course, were meager and there were few other options."

"Blithers' folks seemed to be as worried about violence and the instability of the economy as we are, but he says the men started taking labor jobs in the bigger lumber mills and railroad yards and making baskets at night. The womenfolk were setting up businesses as seamstresses and laundresses. Some of them are growing vegetables to sell. Blithers and a couple of others from the Clotilde voyage went to their previous owners to try to get them to give the Africans some land since they had no place to go, but the landowners said that since they were freedmen now, they owed them nothing. The newly freed began saving the little money they were earning and pooled it together as a group or a community— kind of like their own savings bank. By pooling their money they believed they could make progress toward the purchase of land, and Kate, that's what they are doing, buying one piece of land at a time.

"When they had the amount of money they believed significant, they went back to the landowners and purchased a parcel of land where they could set up their own town. These first seven acres were the beginning. Blithers said the Africans felt a great burden of uncertainty regarding what life would hold in Alabama, but with money so hard to come by, the logical thing seemed to be to stick together and work to preserve some part of their heritage. For the most part, they were a group that kept to themselves and worked pretty good together, despite their being from different African countries and backgrounds. They did have the shared experience of the *Clotilde* voyage, and the 11 days they were made to hide in the swamps as they were being sneaked into the slave market as American slaves rather than as the illegally smuggled Africans they were."

"They chose the nobleman from their enslavement on the *Clotilde* to be their leader, since he was the only one they knew to be of royal lineage. I'm glad we broke from all that royal blood hierarchy, but I guess the Africans needed some variable to support their decision making. Because the Negroes were devastated about not being able to return to their homelands, they called the new settlement Africatown."

"You heard of it?"

"No, I haven't."

"It's new. Maybe you know this Kate, but I never really thought about citizenship for the former slaves. The way I understand it, even though the Negroes were stranded in Alabama and other states and could not leave the country, they had to go through the same process that immigrants go through to become citizens."

"Blithers said he was a fisherman back in Africa; in fact, he was named after a river that ran through his country, but I don't remember what that was. It was unusual, you know—African. He said that is why he came to the Escatawpa, said it was as close as he could get to his home in Africa."

"Blithers said he still misses his home terribly—he calls it 'Afriky soil'—but he watched the destruction of his village and said he must look, not to the painful past, but ahead where he hopes he can find joy. It has been six years now since his capture. He was to have been married just days after his capture, and he has no clue what happened to the woman. He now plans to marry a woman who also came from Africa on the same voyage as he did. Together, they plan to live in Africatown."

"Yeah, Blithers said he was just days away from getting married when his village was raided in the early morning hours, just before dawn. He calls the Dahomey tribe cowards for attacking in the night."

John paused and looked at Kate directly, "What happened next was truly heinous."

"Go ahead," she said.

"There was some sort of traitor situation, where a soldier in the army of Blither's village went to the King of Dahomey, who was already itching to take the village of Blithers' and described the passageways in and out of the settlement. As the villagers slept, Dahomey warriors were posted at each of the eight entrances. The women fighters were positioned within the village and were very adept at tearing the heads off people.

"As the warriors beat down the main gate to create a disturbance, the people who were startled awake began to run about here and there and were consequently beheaded by the women. Blithers, who of course was called by some other name at that time, was captured at the gate and bound, as were many of the young people of the village. The Dahomey warriors carried the heads of villagers with them as trophies of war, including one of the Kings of Takkoi. Marching the captives back to Dahomey took several days. After the severed heads had begun to smell, the soldiers stopped to mount them on sticks and smoked them for nine days for better preservation."

"After three days, Blithers and the other captives were moved from Dahomey to the sea, a place called *Dwhydah*. This is where Blithers says he saw a white man for the first time. He said he had heard of them but had never seen one before. *Whydah* is what the Whites called it. They were in the stockades for three weeks before the white man came with two men from Dahomey, including one that Blithers called a 'word-changer' meaning 'translator.' The Africans were looked over and divided into groups for various slavers. This time was sad for the captured people as they knew they were being separated from the alliances and the friends they made during their capture."

"The captives, who were taken to the *Clotilde*, were hidden deep within the darkness of the boat and were not allowed to come on deck until the 13th day. Blithers said the sound of the ocean waves reaching into the bowels of the ship was fearsome and sounded like a thousand beasts signaling the end of the world. He had no reference for the sound of the ocean until this experience. They questioned where they were going that was so far away. Why was this happening to them? What would happen next? These questions, which seem so familiar to us today, were asked."

"Of grave importance to Blithers was that I understood the captives' clothes had been taken from them when they were put on the boat. He said he could not bear hearing, another time, his people referred to as naked savages. Their clothes had been taken from them."

"In part to hide the human cargo, their time aboard the ship was expanded. The *Clotilde* did not come ashore for 45 days."

"The captives organized and unloaded the ship, after which the ship was burned at sea. The captives then walked for 11 days through the swamp before they were again divided into groups among four plantations."

"It's a strange time Kate. You got Africans who don't even want to be in the United States breaking their backs to get a little piece of land to stand on, and folks like us who have lived in the South all our lives, now looking for a new place to start over. I guess I've told you all this to say that this is a time when it seems like just about everybody, including some folks you wouldn't even normally consider, are struggling with where to be and how to continue life as we know it. Maybe that's the point Kate, will it continue as we know it?"

"I feel ill at the thought of such a barbaric attack on a sleeping village."

"I know Kate; maybe I shouldn't have told you all of this. but it's war, Kate. What war isn't barbaric?"

John's voice began to trail off. "And, Kate, isn't it funny how of all the things you can remember about a place, a time, an event, sometimes it's the most insignificant memories that stick? As I walked away from Blithers the last time, I noticed a flock of geese way high, flying north. Now, every time I see geese, I think of that conversation."

After several moments of silence, Kate responded in an almost whispered response, "No, I don't think life will continue as we know it."

They stood looking at the disappearing horizon and the two elements—the night sky and sea—seemed to have become one. Kate said a quiet, "Good night," and turned to go up the walkway toward her room.

Notch's Story

On a starless night when the children were restless and the Hall boys, Matthew and Paul, had had about enough of each other and began arguing the way only young brothers can do, Notch pulled them aside to distract them. Several of the other children, being their usual curious selves, noticed the attention the brothers were receiving and interjected themselves directly into the conversation.

"What you doing Mr. Notch? Are you going to give Matthew and Paul a swat for being so rambunctious?"

"No, I'm not going to give them a swat, but I'm going to see if they'd like to hear a story that they have probably never heard before. Would you like to gather up close and hear it too? It's about two brothers who didn't get along so well."

The children formed a semicircle on the floor near Notch, and when they settled down, and he had their undivided attention, Notch began, "Way before the time of my great grandfather, there was a tribe of migrating people—that means the people spent much of their time moving from place to place."

"Like us?" Paul questioned.

"Yes, somewhat like us, but this story takes place such a long time ago that no one knows the name this group of people went by —like Scots, Irish, English, French, African and Choctaw."

"And Americans!" Matthew shouted.

"And Americans. These traveling people entered the modern world at a huge mound called Nanih Waiya. Nania Waiya is in Mississippi, just an hour or so horseback ride outside of Philadelphia, Mississippi."

"Philadelphia, Mississippi! I ain't never heard of that!"

Notch took a deep breath and locked eyes with the 11-year-old who seemed to get the message that it was time to settle down. "Just because you've never heard of it, doesn't mean it's not a real place."

"Yeah, you big dummy," Paul said as he shook Matthew's knee, "just because you haven't heard of it doesn't mean it ain't so."

Notch shook his head at the younger brother, cautioning him not to stoke his brother's excitability. "As the people exited the mound, which was nearly 30 feet high, and peered at each other, looking for guidance in this new world, they focused their attention on a pair of brothers who were strong and usually considered very smart–Chata and Chiksa."

Notch paused for a moment thinking he'd hear of a chorus of "I ain't never heard of those names," but the children had settled into the story, so Notch began to embellish. "The brothers believed that there was a big storm coming and both knew they needed to protect the people who were looking up to them, but they didn't agree about the best method of protection.

Chata believed they should stay put, instructing the people to look in the nearby area for nuts and berries and greens that they could survive on until the storm passed. He believed that they could use the mound for protective covering. But, Chiksa thought the people should go further east and attempt to move out of the storm's way. The brothers argued so that the people began to take sides. Chata's followers in the larger group would remain in place with Chata and become known as the Choctaws. The smaller group that moved on eastward, following Chiksa, became known as the Chikasaws."

"That's great! Each brother had his own tribe. That made each of them a chief!"

"You're right my little friend, the brothers did each have their own tribe and become chiefs, but they lost many members of their family, and they each lost their brother's love. This loss makes my heart sad."

Paul grabbed his brother's arm, "Let's not fight. I'd rather have you for my brother than be a chief." Matthew smiled at Notch, "That was a great story, Mr. Notch!"

A little later, Notch met Kate as he headed to his compartment.

"Kate, I've just told some of the children the creation story of the Choctaw people, which as you well know, has nothing to do with Genesis, so if you hear that I'm being thrown overboard, please do come to my rescue!" He chuckled.

"You've done what? And here I thought you were along to look after me. Now I have to watch out for you." They both laughed.

"Well, I didn't say creation or Genesis, or 'in the beginning,' I just jumped right into the version of the story with the two brothers arguing."

"Good for that. You know about 100% of our fellow travelers have belief systems that aren't open to many variables."

"I know that Kate. In those conversations, I probably fit in as well as you do."

"I look forward to the day when the children get to watch you charm some innocent creature right into your palm." Over the years, Kate had seen Notch wait-out lizards and the like until they crawled into the palm of his hand. She'd never seen anyone but Notch, be so still—peaceful and patient, aligned with the natural world. "Surely, there's got to be a critter you can lure into your hands somewhere on this boat. You said you were headed to your room?"

"Yes."

"My brain has been too busy today. I know it's darker than usual on deck tonight but walk just a circle or two around with me, if you will. Maybe that'll help quiet my mind."

Notch took her hand in his and turned them both around for a stroll.

On deck, the two ran into John Foster smoking his evening cigar. He smelled of cherry and honey, which was not unpleasant to Kate. "Why don't you two join me?" he invited as he exhaled and crushed the lit end of the cigar. Kate felt he'd smothered the fire of his cigar in deference to her, so she led the way to the side chairs.

"Don't think of my questions as an interrogation, but I'm curious about you Notch. What's your persuasion? As in, where are you from, who's your family?"

Given the previous conversation that she and Notch had just had, Kate realized how fast information traveled. She asked, "Are you upset or concerned about something Mr. Foster?"

"No, just genuinely interested, I've heard talk that you're Indian, and it's been such a long and boring day, I could really use the company, and the information is always good."

"I don't mind Foster. Well, where to start?"

"You seem better educated than the average fella—White or Indian; how's that?

"Education has always been essential to my family. I attended the University of Nashville for a few years before the war. My uncle, you may have heard of him, Greenwood LeFlore, was also educated in Nashville, not at the university, but privately. "

"Leflore, that's French or something, right?"

"You've got it. My grandfather was Louis Lefleur, a French-Canadian fur trader. In the United States, he worked for a company called Panton, Leslie & Company based in Florida, and did a lot of trading with the individual Choctaw tribes before they were organized into what we now call the Choctaw Nation. He was a very industrious and wise man who established a trading post over on the Pearl River. The fact that he was a smart fella is evident in his decision to marry my grandmother Rebecca, who was a high-ranking niece of the great Choctaw chief Pushmataha.

"You see my great uncle Pushmataha is known as the greatest of Choctaw chiefs. He earned his reputation by being skilled at both war and diplomacy. My great uncle's reputation in Washington was important to Louis Lefleur, but equally or maybe more important, was the fact that in the Choctaw world, status is transferred through the women, so my grandmother's marriage to Lefleur is what garnered the Frenchman significant power and respect. There was precedence for Rebecca marrying a Frenchman as her mother, my great-grandmother, had done the same. For a long time, my people —the Choctaw—have understood that the world, as our ancestors knew it, was changing and changing rapidly. Most ethnic groups resist intermarriage with other groups, being fearful of tainting the pure bloodlines and such nonsense. "

"Nonsense?"

"That's not how the Choctaw see it; they recognized that intermarriage could help the Choctaw people navigate the New World, to gain recognition and hold power. You know my Uncle Greenwood just passed away last year—he was a good man, but not everyone thought so. Sometimes he made the mistake of trusting the wrong people, but he did what he thought was best for the people. No one can see the future. Everyone is deceived some time or another. There's never a time when everyone sees a thing the same way."

"I know the French explored Mississippi and Alabama, Florida and all, but to be truthful, I never thought about them intermarrying with the Indians, no disrespect intended to you Notch. So, is that name of yours Choctaw?"

"My name has a bit of a humorous origin. My mother and father had trouble agreeing on a name for me. It was a season of several births in our community, and all the good names were being spoken for fast. As the story goes, when my mother delivered my father a thriving baby, he took one look at the fine boy and said, 'This one is a notch above the rest.' My father wouldn't refer to me in any other way, and eventually, my mother acquiesced as she watched him dote over me. I take it seriously, you know, being a notch above the rest and all."

John looked as if he wasn't exactly sure how to respond. Notch couldn't hold his expression any longer and laughed aloud. "Come on Foster, lighten up. It's alright to have a little fun, even at my expense."

John laughed, "Well, it's a mighty fine name, a little unusual, but mighty fine."

"As I said, we don't all see things the same way, which wasn't only applicable to the Choctaw. The French had their own perspective of things as well, unlike the English, no disrespect intended to you Foster, the French were less interested in trying to change or subjugate my ancestors and more interested in doing business with them. The trading, particularly the fur trading, had high value to both sides."

"You can see the perspective in the language."

"What do you mean?"

"The Choctaw have a name for these mixed-race children — like my mother and uncle, myself — it's *itibapishii toba*, which essentially means to become brothers or sisters, which is a cherished relationship."

"Brothers and sisters?"

"The Choctaw and, in this case, French are considered brothers and sisters through this bloodline."

"Foster, my story is simply my story. I know that I'm fortunate to have lived among the elite and have the privilege of Choctaw bloodline and White education. I know this combination of characteristics makes me an oddity to some. Many of my Choctaw relations who stayed in Mississippi after the Treaty at Dancing Rabbit Creek ended up being sharecroppers; a few became merchants. Now that you know I'm Choctaw, you see me, and you see Choctaw. I'm Choctaw and proud of my heritage, but much of my appearance could also be from my French descendants; that is, the dark eyes, black hair, my less-than-tall height. Labeling people is an interesting process, isn't it Foster?"

"Well, I don't believe the races ought to mix. And, I believe that's based in the word of the Lord—in the Bible. Now, I won't hold that against you Notch, but it's what I believe."

Kate interjected, "Maybe it's time to move along in this conversation or call it quits for the evening."

Foster shifted in his chair and smiled at Kate. "Yes Ma'am, we're going to be civil. So, tell me more about Leflore. He was high up in state government, wasn't he? I've heard of him."

"Yes, Uncle Greenwood took on leadership roles when he was in his early twenties as President Andrew Jackson was getting all riled up with the Indian Removal Act. Previously, the Choctaw leaders led smaller geographic regions of people, but they could see that they needed to unite to be a stronger voice in the negotiations. My uncle searched for various ways to legislatively resist the Concept of Removal, even though he felt certain that there was no way to stop it. He encouraged his followers to build permanent homes, grow crops, send their children to schools, and to convert to Christianity. He even drafted a treaty and sent it to Washington DC."

"You don't convert to Christianity because someone directs you to do so." Foster shook his head. "Becoming a Christian is the work of the Lord in a man's heart."

"I'm trying to explain Amoshi. By the way, that's what we called him. It's the Choctaw word for uncle. Amoshi believed the best tactic for the Choctaw people to be able to stay in their ancient homeland was by merging into the larger culture that was taking over at an incredible rate."

"Go on."

"The treaty that Greenwood sent to Washington included a reservation of land for each head of a family. If I remember correctly, the land to be reserved was just over 600 acres. Then there were additional amounts awarded for children of the family based on age. The treaty was agreed upon, but the implementation went very badly, as is so often the case. The agent representing the United States refused to sign the people up for their land, which undermined my uncle's objective. The agent wanted all full-bloodied Choctaw out of the region, and by doing a worse than sloppy job at registering families, he achieved his goal. Some of the people grew to despise Amoshi, but I do believe that everything he did was in good faith. It's true that my uncle received about 1,000 acres of land and included in the calculation was a consideration of my cousins living with him at the time."

"It's getting late, but I'll add that my uncle did become a wealthy planter. 15 or so years ago, he built a beautiful home that he called *Malmaison*. Amoshi greatly admired the French architectural elements, and he commissioned an architect from Georgia to design his home after Napoleon and Josephine Bonaparte's home near Paris, which they called *Chateau de Malmaison*. Uncle's home was a beautiful replication with grand columns and several iron balconies. I lived, with my parents, on the edge of his land and we visited *Malmaison* often. Uncle had 400 African slaves who worked the cotton fields of his plantation. He was a close friend of Jefferson Davis, but ironically, sided with the Federal government in the war. He was a diverse and interesting character, that's for sure. Did you know that he not only became a U.S. citizen, but he was buried wrapped in an American flag?"

"He owned slaves?"

"Yes, he did. Many of them remained in the area after they were freed."

"So, Notch, you were on the Yankee side in the war?"

"I never said that. My engagement in that war was to do what I could do at the so-called medical facilities and prisons along the coast. I helped to patch up all kinds."

There was a brief silence. Foster had a lot of information to mull over.

Southern Cross and Pernambuco

Notch and Kate sat together on the deck of the *Isabella* watching a marvelous full moon. "Can you see your rabbit in the moon, Kate?"

Kate started and looked in all directions. "Notch, that's a secret! You promised as my best childhood friend that you would never say a word about that!"

"Kate, most of your family and friends think you're crazy for taking this voyage. Your idea of seeing a rabbit in the face of the moon as a child is small potatoes to this lark of yours."

"It was just so odd to be unable to see the man in the moon, which filled nursery stories, and everyone talked about, but to see something that I'd never heard anyone else speak of. I knew it was unusual and thought it best to keep that vision to myself."

"Ahh, Kate, it wasn't a vision, but a perspective and that is precisely one of the things I like so much about you. Your perspective is usually different from the crowd. There's a lot to be said for being able to see something from a different perspective."

"It's funny how incidents and stories get stuck in the mind and take on a life of their own. I miss my Father and the stories he'd tell about his childhood, how things were and all. Sometimes he'd tell a fantasy, but I think, maybe as a child, I interpreted the fantasy to be something that had happened years ago, in his childhood or before that. Right now, I'm thinking specifically of how we'd walk across his place in the early evening, checking for what might be blooming and on the ripening scuppernongs, which were anxiously awaited as he loved to make scuppernong jelly to go with breakfast biscuits. Well, he loved biscuits anytime."

"Anyway, he'd point out the fog rising in the valley and say, 'Look, Lilly Kate, the rabbits are cooking their supper,' the idea being, of course, that the fog was smoke from the cooking fires. Even today when I see fog in a river bottom or across a field, I think to myself, 'Ah the rabbits are at it again.'"

"Notch, where would I've been without you as my friend all these years and now this trip?"

Captain Briggs approached the two. "Mrs. Teal, Mr. Notch, tonight is one for the journals you travelers write."

"Captain, it's one for our diaries; this full moon is extraordinary, especially as we stand here on deck, while we float in the massive ocean by the light of its bright face."

"Yes, Ma'am, but, also, I want to point out what you might miss without a little extra direction. We have sailed far enough south now that we sailors rely on the Southern Cross for navigation."

"The Southern Cross?"

"Yes, Ma'am. The lines aren't as clear as one might imagine, but this evening is cause for a toast, as we've slipped out of the realm of the North Star and into the realm of the Southern Cross. We're near the latitude of the equator. We probably crossed over a day or so back. When old sailors crossed into the southern hemisphere, they began relying on the Southern Cross to steer by, as the North Star and the Big Dipper, a constellation that most in the northern hemisphere are aware of, has disappeared."

"You've only missed its most spectacular presence by a few weeks. The constellation shows its absolute brightest in March and early April, but now is still a good time." The captain pointed to the night sky. "See that bright bluish star up there? That's what some folks call the Bluish Crux. It's the brightest star in the Southern Cross constellation. Now, trace a line upward at a slight angle, and you'll see the star the Latins called Gacrux. If you trace a line from Gacrux to Bluish Crux, the direction will lead you straight to the Southern Celestial Pole. Straightaway, if you look just about halfway up this imaginary line that we've drawn, on the left side you'll see another bright star, not as bright as Bluish Crux, but second to it. This is Beta Crux. The Germans call it Mimosa, but I find that confusing. So, slanting upward, crossing our original imaginary line you see Beta Crux and almost directly across from it, here, you see Delta Crux. These four stars form the constellation. Can you see it?"

Notch saw it immediately. He stood behind Kate and cupped her head in his hands, tilting it slightly. After a bit of a struggle, Kate finally said quietly, "Yes, yes, I can."

Notch smiled.

"Seems good to be sailing under a constellation by that name. It's like a good sign."

The captain chuckled, "Sometimes we can see the Southern Cross as far north as St. Thomas or even the tip of Florida, but certainly by this point, it's our singular guide. Having this beautiful calm night for sailing is indeed a good sign. Good evening, to you two."

As Notch took his leave, Kate settled back in her favorite deck chair and continued the star gazing and moon observation. While Kate's mind was usually full, she was excellent at being able to let all her thoughts go and to be caught in the moment. She wasn't sure how much time had passed before John Foster walked directly to her and asked to join her.

"What's going on in that pretty little head of yours?"

Kate was happy that it was dark enough on deck to hide her blushing cheeks. She'd already concluded that John was a flatterer, who enjoyed throwing compliments about and was somewhat of a teaser, which was enough to keep her off balance. She never knew whether his comments were serious or frivolous.

"Well, to tell you the truth and I'm not sure why I'm inclined to do so, I was thinking more about perspective. Notch and I were having a conversation about this before the Captain joined us earlier this evening to explain The Southern Cross constellation." Kate rushed forward to explain the constellation about which she'd learned. John was aware of it but didn't know all the details Kate shared with him.

"So Kate, what do all these details about the Southern Cross constellation have to do with perspective?"

"Oh yes, I was saying that I'm not sure why I'm inclined to share details with you that, for the most part, I've held close. Maybe I just care less about other people's perception of me these days."

"You appear to me to be a brave and confident woman who could care less about what other people think."

"Perhaps that is the truth, but I've been long in realizing it myself."

"I'm still curious about perception and the conversation you were having with Notch."

"Oh yes! Notch and I were chatting about the rabbit in the moon."

"The what?"

"According to Notch since most people who know me think I'm off my rocker anyway, I don't suppose it could hurt to tell you the truth about the rabbit in the moon. I declare John. I don't know why I trust you. For what it's worth, as a child, I could never see the proverbial man in the moon, but what I did see was a rabbit in the moon. I knew this vision wasn't normal, so I kept it to myself. Well, I told Notch of course, but no one else. Tonight, as we were naming constellations, he asked me about any lunar sightings of the rabbit in the moon.

"Is it there this evening?"

"But of course. Here, let me show you." Kate carefully first pointed out the long ears as they curved around the upper portion of the moon's arc, then the little-pointed nose and round belly.

"Have you ever seen the rabbit in the moon?"

"Nope, I can't say that I have, not until this moment, but I do now."

"I've learned that there are indigenous people of Mexico who have myths about a rabbit in the moon. Also, Asian cultures. Isn't that just fascinating?"

Before he could stop her, she went on to a new question.

"Do you read"? Kate asked.

John pretended to be insulted, and while he was quite good at holding a straight face, the single dimple of his right cheek gave in as his eyes met hers directly, "Well, yeah I read!"

She smiled, a little frustrated at having the point of her story interrupted, but she knew she'd brought it on herself.

"I mean do you read literature and the like? I've been thinking about that naïve, lovestruck Juliette Capulet in the famous Shakespearian play. For all her youth and innocence, she understood that life isn't constant. It's not so predictable as we might have thought it to be. Is it? The girl in the play said 'O, swear not by the moon, the fickle moon, the inconstant moon, that monthly changes in her circle orb, lest that thy love prove likewise variable.'"

Kate knew that she couldn't even count on the spin of the earth. "It feels like that now, doesn't it, John — that there's little to count on? Did you know that last February there was no full moon? They say it's the only time in recorded history that there was a month with no full moon. What do you think that means? It must mean something."

"The girl's right. I know it for a fact. Did you know that moon rise takes place nearly an hour later each day?"

"No, I wasn't aware of that. I know that I look for the moon regularly, and sometimes I find it, sometimes I don't. Sometimes it's in vastly different places, even though the time of evening might be the same."

"Well, there you go with the fickleness. Kate, I don't know the scientific reasoning, but I've learned that the new moon always rises at sunrise, the first quarter moon rises at noon, the last quarter moon rises at midnight. Now, that information should come in handy for your moon gazing activities!"

"It will. Thanks, Mr. Foster."

As Kate walked away, she was thinking of how familiar the two of them had become and how natural it seemed—all the confiding, chatting, and teasing. She'd forgotten to worry about decorum and decided not to start.

Captain Briggs anchored *Isabella* just off the mainland of Pernambuco, in northeastern Brazil, where they would stay for the next four days while provisions for the remainder of the trip were loaded. Of importance again, was fresh drinking water and coal fuel. John was always interested in detail and engaged First Officer Bennett in conversation regarding the calculation procedures for coal quantities with consideration for wind currents and weight.

As the steamer's crew was given its clearance, John departed the boat at about 2 p.m. with some of his new seafaring friends to spend the next three hours exploring. The city was divided into three sections—San Pedro, Racife, and San Antonio or Boa Vista. The river Beberibe separated the three. John couldn't believe that one river could manage to separate the three sections of the city so completely. He was intrigued by four tremendous bridges that connected each section to the other and marveled at their width of

200 feet. They were as fine as any bridges he'd ever seen. Under his breath, he remarked several times, "Now, isn't that something?"

The group of urban explorers returned to the city's central district and joined Major Hall and some of the other travelers for dinner at a progressive French Restaurant.

The following day John was duly impressed by the high quality and significant quantity of cotton, bound in round bales, being moved down the cobbled streets through town in a single line, one or two bales to a cart pulled by small horses. John was pleased to see that this cotton was comparable to the best cotton in Alabama and Mississippi. There was indeed money to be made in Brazil.

Pernambuco seemed to be experiencing what the southerners call a rainy spell. There'd been almost constant rain for two or three weeks, and while the water level of the converging rivers was indeed high, the center of the city was undisturbed except for the additional crowding caused by many people of the lowlands seeking refuge in the city from flooding in the outlying areas.

Although John was anxious to continue with the trip, he dreaded re-boarding the boat as he hadn't managed the sailing experience as well as he thought he might. Back on the ship, sailing out of Pernambuco, he succumbed to the fever and chills he'd heard some of the locals speak of. He mingled very little with the other passengers for the four-plus days that it took to sail to Rio de Janeiro.

When John felt more like himself again, he went on deck to find that Cape Frio was to the north and land was in sight again. The view of land helped him gain his full composure.

John drew a deep breath, marveling at the beauty of the Rio Harbor. The water was deep enough to admit the largest of ships, and there were dozens in the harbor from points throughout the world. In the distance to the west, he could see the Peaks of the Organ Mountains, named that because they resembled the pipes of an organ. John breathed deeply and felt renewed excitement about the adventure ahead.

SEARCHING

Hotel Exchange in Rio

As many of the passengers from the *Isabella* crowded into the lobby of the Hotel Exchange in Rio, Kate looked for a spot away from the hub of activity and was drawn to a vast table topped with a round slab of pink granite that must have been eight feet or more in diameter. In the middle of the table stood a floral arrangement at least three feet tall. To Kate, it was a work of art dotted with exotic strokes of purple, orange and yellow bird-of-paradise. For the longest time, she tried to name another bloom when she realized that what she was looking at was feathery, opening buds of yellow irises. The recognition brought her great delight, and she laughed aloud at herself. The arrangement was anchored with light purple agapanthus pomes and whimsical, twisting tangerine trumpet vines that matched with golden puffs, much like a dense dandelion. Orange sprays extended outward from their soft centers and were accented with complementing soft red cones of achiote. It was a universe of color, shape, and texture within itself.

She was almost sure that at least a portion of the green filler was sugar cane, and another greenery was palm. Pencil-thin bamboo stakes stabilized the explosion of color. As she surveyed the rest of the lobby, she saw that it was filled with fresh cut arrangements of various sizes and dimensions. Kate was immersed in them and felt that each deserved close examination to see what surprises it might hold—like the newly budding irises. She wondered how many people noticed the arrangements singularly, apart from the sweeping beauty of the lobby in its entirety, and then of those, how many saw the uniqueness in each. One side table held a bouquet of ivory roses mingled with curling brown stem accents. Near the café entrance, a tall clear vase was filled with lemons, yellow lilies, wide leaves of variegated yellow ginger, and orchids. She'd never actually seen orchids, and here the lobby was scattered with the blooms, displaying exotic petals, long throats, and fragrances of rose and vanilla. The detail was intriguing, and she wondered about the artist behind such displays. She felt her life was at its best when she could see the details in front of her.

These fleeting moments in the hotel lobby she took as a good sign.

Notch assisted Kate with getting her trunks to her room as she anticipated the hotel would be her living quarters for some time to come. She set about making the space work for her. As soon as she'd arranged the few possessions that she needed most frequently, she'd begin exploring the city and looking for employment. She presumed that the immigrants would be looking for schools for their children, and she felt she just needed to find pockets of U.S. citizens to make the best connections. Kate wasn't always so confident, but she was so sure this was the right move for her that she hardly winced at the thought of coming so far without a previously arranged agreement for a job.

São Paulo

Kate had learned that the São Paulo region was the place where many of the Americanos, one of the names the locals referred to the influx of people from the southern states of the U.S., had established new homes. She felt her search for a teaching position might go well there, so she didn't hesitate to accept John's invitation for her to come along with the group which was headed out to scout the countryside for land for homesteads. Rio was more than double the size of New Orleans and more challenging to navigate. Kate felt that she would have better direct access to community leaders in São Paulo, a community of about 20,000, a fraction of the population in Rio. After being in Rio de Janeiro for almost a full month, she said her goodbyes to Notch and boarded the afternoon train.

As John stepped aboard the train, he was filled with energy and assisted Kate with her bags. Kate was surprised at how quickly she became integrated into the group of gentlemen who were on the advanced edge of the scouting mission. The air was charged with excitement and anticipation.

Kate felt comfortable traveling with the group, and in fact, was happy to continue in the company of some of those with whom she'd traveled from Boston and others she'd met in Rio. However, since she wasn't an official part of that expedition and had only been on the fringes of the official scouting conversations, she knew about their tasks through her lengthy conversations with John. He seemed happy to have her along, so she relaxed into the journey ahead.

"Well Kate, I've looked around, high and low, and see no cushions to make this ride more comfortable anywhere on this train. It's going to be a long afternoon."

The passenger cars were small and divided further into compartments that held about 10 people each. Kate glanced around and noticed that no seats within her sight had cushions.

"We'll be fine, I'm sure."

There she was again, accepting what came her way. John was almost bewildered by her ability to accept life as it came to her. Sure, the lack of seat cushions was a simple inconvenience, but her acceptance of discomfort seemed to be indicative of her attitude towards life. John didn't say it, but he knew that Cynthia would've complained the entire trip about the absence of cushions.

"Being a bit of an engineer myself, I must say I'm a bit disappointed in the construction of these train cars. I understand that they were built by Englishmen and with English capital. You'd think they would be of higher quality than they are. I guess the main thing is that they get us to São Paulo."

John began filling Kate in on recent details that supported the trip. "We're traveling with a letter of introduction from the Brazilian Minister of Agriculture, who made a very generous offer to pay our hotel bill, as well as our transportation fees. As a group, we felt the offer too much and accepted only the transportation fare, which is what we had been promised in earlier correspondence back and forth with the Brazilian consulate before we set out from the United States. His underlings met us at the train station and paid the rail fee for all of us. He didn't seem to mind that we had an extra passenger or two." He winked at Kate. "Major Hall is holding the letters for us, and Mr. Grafton has gone ahead to make our hotel arrangements for the stay in São Paulo. I've asked him to arrange a room for you at the same hotel as well. No need in you wandering around to make those arrangements after we get in this evening."

Kate had to be mindful of her budget, but she agreed that she needed a place from which to go forth and familiarize herself with the new city.

The terrain changed dramatically over the slow afternoon ride, starting on an incline 2100 feet above sea level. Passenger cars were pulled by four engines attached by a large rope made of wire. A telegraph was used to alert the first engine that the passengers were settled, and they were off. After the path leveled off, they traveled the first 13 miles over a low marshy ground covered with a thick stunted growth of trees and shrubs. Numerous unusual botanic parasites filled the larger trees. Many of the trees with expansive branches were covered with large red blooms.

As the noisy cars started up the mountainside, the conversation with John became more difficult and limited, but Kate endeavored anyway.

"Did you hear that the red blooms in those trees we saw earlier are prized in Rio and sell for as much as 30 American dollars a stem? I think they're called Royal Poinciana. I fell in love with the beautiful floral arrangements in the hotels and public buildings in Rio, but I had no idea they were as precious to the local folks as they were to me. Think of all the other things you could buy for that kind of money! But, oh how exotic and beautiful! I'm so practical when it comes to money, even when I don't have to be, but maybe beauty is worth the price."

John smiled, thinking to himself how uniquely beautiful she was and how lucky a man would be to wake up to her smile every day. Passing through the mountain gorges, Kate was the first to point to the red soil and saw smiles on her traveling companions' faces at the similarity to the red dirt clay banks of the Tuscaloosa Trend in Alabama, Georgia, and Mississippi.

They arrived in São Paulo at about 5 p.m., but the railway workers labored nearly two hours, sorting through the baggage and loading it on a mule-driven cart. The party of *Confederados*, another name by which the travelers from the southern states were called, and a few others, proceeded on foot to the Europa Hotel.

They were a talkative bunch as they made their way and anticipated the next step of their journey. Mr. Grafton successfully secured suitable rooms for all of them. The gentlemen saw their bags to their rooms, then returned downstairs for dinner and to solidify their plans for the next few days. John was one of the last to push back from his seat, where the men had sat together smoking cigars, and head for his room. As he passed the kitchen, he saw Kate and immediately approached her.

"Kate, excuse me, are you well?"

She was startled and clasped the small covered plate more tightly in her hand. "Good evening, John. Yes, I'm well. I thought I'd be fine without an evening meal but found that I couldn't go to sleep without a little something to carry me over till morning, so I came down and did my best to ask the kitchen help for a cold biscuit or something similar. I thought I was doing an acceptable job with my request, but one of the hotel workers who spoke a smidgen of English heard the exchange and came over to assist." Bemused, she said, "I believe what I have on my little plate here is called *broa*, which may be a cornmeal and rye flour mixture. I'm sure it'll fill the hunger.

John smiled, as Kate continued, "I'm a bit concerned with my lack of ability to speak any Portuguese at all." Suddenly, she blushed, realizing that she was walking in circles around him as she talked. She was intrigued by him, but apparently, her subconscious was not sure of his intentions.

John reached down and squeezed her hands clasped around the small plate. "Kate, why don't you come sit down in the lobby, and I'll sit with you while you have your 'biscuit?'" He directed her to a pair of blue-tufted chairs near the window. "Let me see if I can find a little something for you to drink."

John returned shortly with a cup of *cafe zinho* with sugar which suited her well. When their eyes met, she laughed aloud, and he joined in the laughter. "Why're you laughing, John Foster?"

"Because you are! The sound of your laughter is quite refreshing. I thought you might be laughing at this tiny coffee cup, but it's what the kitchen workers insisted on, and my negotiation skills did not prove beneficial. Be careful; it's very hot. While you eat your 'biscuit,' and have your tiny cup of coffee why don't you tell me what you're going to do here in São Paulo."

"Well, John, I already feel more comfortable here than in the larger city of Rio.. Thank you for suggesting the change of venue and for making the arrangements, including seeing that my fare was paid. I admit that I have serious concerns about the language barrier, but I'm going to be brave and get busy learning some basic words while you gentlemen are working with the government to secure your homesteads. I suppose, there aren't any government stipends to help relocate teachers for American families, I'll be looking to meet as many English-speaking families who may have preceded us here as I can in hopes of locating or perhaps creating a teaching position."

"I'm a pretty positive guy, but Kate, I have to tell you, your penchant for the positive inspires me, makes me feel like a young man."

Kate noticed that rain was beginning to fall softly against the doorway and diverted the compliment, which was something of a skill she'd practiced and been teased about in her younger years. "John, look its beginning to rain." Her tone became nostalgic as she spoke. "I can remember cold as a very young child, but I have no memory of rain until I was about 10 years old. What I remember is bright white lightning that hissed and crackled like the center of the earth was splitting, followed by the sky darkening and thunder clouds slamming together with a force that made the house shudder.

Some thundershowers stirred up every afternoon in summer, disrupting any productivity, including what was happening indoors —picking over shelled purple hull peas for trash, insects, and the like, stitching a winter quilt for insurance against a very different kind of day or whatever. All work just stopped, the field cultivation stopped, the blacksmithing to create a new iron latch for the gate stopped, even the circular journey of the old mules squeezing stalks for cane juice. All industry stopped as if to pay homage to, but more likely in fear of, the great Lord our God whom we may not have pleased.

Maybe the quiet that overcame the fields and kitchens was in simple awe of the powerful energy beyond the control of mortals. While most of the people in my immediate surroundings were brought up to believe that God is in control, it was difficult for responsible, hard-working people not to try to control most everything. These storms seemed like mixtures of nature's afternoon tantrums.

Nature slammed against what was built by men, burned their barns, caused iron bed posts to act as lightning conductors, and created ear-splitting strikes. Once the center part of a coarse rug that covered the uneven yellow pine floorboards of my grandmother's bedroom was seared by a lightning strike. I've heard tell of those incidents, but for me, I've only seen a cedar tree split in half with a single strike, creating an ear-splitting cracking. The interior wood was left jagged, and its base splintered open, it's rough texture in shades of yellow and orange looking like flames themselves."

"As children, we were required to sit still and quiet until the storm passed, as if we should hide from it. Now, I rush to the porch to watch the shifting clouds form a dark canopy in the sky, feel the wind stir, smell the rain approaching, and feel my heart rattle with the thunder. I'm excited by these clamoring elements. They make me feel fully present and whole."

John watched her intently as she spoke. He loved how she could get excited about the simplest things, how profound they were to her, how she could describe with such detail. He understood it and found joy in the fact that rain was no longer an imposition in the day's work, but a reminder of how it felt to be alive.

"So, this is something familiar for us—rain!" He followed her to the door as she adjusted the wrap around her shoulders, leaning in with no compunction, and stopping her in mid-sentence, he said firmly, "I could fall in love with you."

She paused only momentarily, her quizzical blue eyes locking his as she said, "Well, that will never happen. This is how it'll be, we'll share interests, but there's no need to complicate the relationship further. It can be done. I have many friends who are men."

John stepped out under the eaves to ensure that the cover from the rain was adequate and reached for her hand to lead her out, keeping her back next to the wall. They stood, without exchanging a word and watched the few pedestrians still scampering for cover into doorways on either side of the street.

"I find the fact that you like to watch the rain reassuring in some way, Kate."

Before she could reply, he took her chin in his hand, lifted her mouth to his, and kissed her warmly, softly, thoroughly. Her mouth met his as if he'd reached for her thousands of times. The kiss was so natural and easy that she didn't think to pull away; in fact, she might have leaned in. John put his hand at her waist and guided her back inside.

Kate knew there was another kind of storm brewing, and it caused her mind to become very still as if she were again watching for the approach of a thing that was out of her control. She shook her head gently as if to clear it physically, returned to the lobby and began asking John specific logistical questions about his upcoming foray into the landscapes of Brazil. He filled her in on the details he knew about, including his goal of finding acreage that would be large enough, not only for the farm he wanted but perhaps for a small settlement. "I better get some shut-eye, now," he said.

They both stood, and he walked her to her hotel room. When he said good night, he turned her face to his and kissed her again. This time, John ran his tongue inside her mouth just across her upper lip, and when she tried to catch her breath, he took a step backward. He gently brushed her cheek with the back of his hand, and she said goodnight. She turned the lock and went inside her cozy room, holding the door as she quietly closed it to the night, John Foster, and the coming storm.

John's Exploratory Journey

John was excited about the forthcoming journey. He had high hope for what lay ahead. His sleep was restless, and when he woke he thought of the kiss with Kate. Perhaps he shouldn't have reached for her, but it seemed like such a natural thing to do. No matter, there was much to do in the day ahead, his first day exploring the countryside.

On Thursday morning, June 26th, John, Major Hall, and Joe Matthews set out to line up logistics and provisions for the scouting expedition. Hall carried the letters of introduction. The visitations were a bit messy as the rain had begun falling again. The group found Dr. Punto not to be in, but Mr. J.J. Aubertin, an Englishman who oversaw a portion of the railroad, was happy to receive the group. He had been advised that the group would be arriving that day, and he welcomed the men with a generous spirit, offering to assist the group in any way that he could.

On Friday morning, Dr. Punto made his way to the hotel and let the group know that he'd arranged a meeting with the President of São Paulo, Saturday, at 11 a.m.

Additionally, Dr. Punto had arranged with Mr. Felix to take the small scouting party on a seven-mile excursion out of São Paulo. For the first part of the journey, they went by open coach, then rode by horseback the remainder of the way, arriving at the *fazenda*, which was much like a small plantation in the U.S. just past noon. They strolled the ten-acre ground stopping often to admire the garden of turnips, cabbage, lettuce, carrots, and some English peas, which the locals called French beans. They noted patches of *coppino*, which is a grape used for livestock fodder. Several agricultural experiments were going on at the site. A half-acre had been planted in rice, which they learned would produce a second crop without replanting. A quarter acre, which seemed a tiny allotment to John, had been planted in sugar cane. It hadn't been planted more than two months, and Mr. Felix had no idea what yield he could anticipate.

They took to their horses again and rode some two and a half miles through a forest on a narrow road, not much more than a path that had been cut through it. The timber was small, but the vines created what John had imagined would be a Brazilian jungle. The guides told stories of monkeys in the forest, but the party didn't see any. John wondered if the crew might be being watched by the monkeys as they strolled along the trail. The trees resembled the Magnolia Bay, wild peach, and Japanese plum trees. Some of the trees resembled Locust, but many trees had a lighter colored bark like the Swamp Red Maple with which John was familiar. The trees were covered with many beautiful parasites, blooms of various hues and shapes suspended from the boughs. Some had roots with short spikes that were used as construction nails called *cipro*. The vine seemed sturdy as rawhide, and the *cipro* was the size of a man's little finger and were exceedingly plentiful. There were also orange and lemon citrus trees.

John was dismayed by the proliferation of ants—several kinds! They made hills that added an undulating appearance to the countryside. Many hills were about a foot high, but they observed some that were a whopping eight feet high with about a 15-foot-wide base. He estimated there to be as many as 200 hills to an acre. The white ant, *formega-copine*, was a distinctive type of ant on the *fazenda* with mounds generally not over three feet high and about 18 inches thick at the base.

John thought the smaller mounds resembled the fields where sweet potatoes are planted in America. He felt these ants would be a nuisance if not detrimental, but the locals said they could easily be destroyed by using a blacksmith's bellow to blow smoke from sulfur and charcoal into the mound, destroying all that encountered the fumes. John observed aloud that it would be quite a serious undertaking to rid a home place of hundreds of acres of an ant population burgeoning to this magnitude.

Then there were the red ants which made mounds three to five feet high with about a foot, maybe a little more at the base. These large red ants frequently had openings in their mounds 40 to 50 yards apart. John had never seen so many ants, and the presence of the mounds, one after another, dismayed him.

After the tour, the team of scouts headed back to Mr. Felix's *fazenda* for a meal before trekking back to São Paulo. The following day, they were scheduled to set out on an expedition that was to last two months.

On Tuesday, July 3, John Foster, Mr. Matthews, and Major Hall set out with an interpreter, Mr. Hesse, and with one mule each to ride and two for carrying their bundles. The animals and the saddles had been purchased for the group by the president of São Paulo.

John questioned the use of the animals, "I would've hoped for a little better riding animal. This mule doesn't hold a candle to my roan, Buttermilk, back home. I guess it's the best they have to lend us from São Paulo."

Dan Hall offered John an explanation, "The bad news on that front, John, is that about eight months ago some character who called himself General Woods came through this province at the expense of the Governor. Woods' spending was considered excessive by the government, and to top it off, they haven't seen Woods since he left. Even though he'd talked of as many as 100,000 families emigrating from the southern states to Brazil, the government hasn't seen the first family because of that expedition. I'm sure the government is somewhat wary after an experience with such an imposter. I don't think any of us even believe that there's going to be a perfect departure from the South."

"Well, we've never made such promises! All that we have said is that we're scouting this territory on behalf of our own families and a few neighbors and that if we find the lands suitable, along with other factors, we might emigrate to Brazil. We didn't say positively that we would settle here," John said.

"So, given the fact that failed promises have preceded us and that our proclamation about what we intend to do is rather small, I tend to think that we should remain in a state of appreciation for the animals that we do have," Mr. Hesse said.

"Agreed! My backside misses Buttermilk, and I expect it will be missing my roan even more by the end of this day," John replied.

The party continued traveling. For the first three or four miles the undulating hills, green foliage of exotic plants, timber and meandering streams, which seemed to be of excellent quality made a good impression on John. After crossing the Tiete River, the land grew hillier, and the soil appeared poorer, as the clay-like soil took on a yellow tint. Anthills continued to be ever-present. Hesse stopped the group around noon, and everyone had water, and a few ate a small portion of food from their packs before heading on to Cotia, a small village of 800 inhabitants. The crew arrived at 5 p.m. at a hotel kept by a Frenchman. John commented, under his breath, that the Frenchman wasn't the neatest innkeeper he'd ever seen, but he was very kind and provided dinner for them and forage for their mules.

It was evident that the people of Cotia were impoverished. Their houses were made of upright posts set in the ground and created a 12-foot square living space. The platforms were secured with the *cipro* wood nails that they'd observed earlier. There seemed to be a real shortage of timber from which to make planks and shingles; consequently, the roof was thatched, and the floors of these small homes were dirt. Their thatched roof had been created from plants that grew along the stream banks. The exterior of some of the other houses was covered with mud plaster, and the roofs were plastered, then covered with tiles. The party was told that the price of the tile was generally at $15 per thousand, and 1,000 tiles covered a room 20 feet square.

By six the next morning, the group had had their coffee at the hotel and was on the road to Sao Rusage, which had about the same number of residents as Cotia. The topography of the 16 miles they covered before noon was full of steep hills, and the road was rough. The area contained clear, rushing mountain springs. While the vegetation of the area was lush and rich, the people, again seemed poor.

Their cattle were plagued by insects they call *bisho*, which can do great harm to the animal it bites. The bite was somewhat like an incision, and after biting, the insects lay eggs in the animal's skin which, in time, resembled maggots. If there was no intervention, the *bisho* maggots continued feeding until the animal died. Intervention meant controlling the spread of the dreaded insects by cutting them and their eggs out of the hide and skin, then rubbing a mercurochrome mixture into the sores.

The team of scouts left Sao Rusage before sunrise and headed through more mountainous territory for Sorocaba. After about a half hour, the group witnessed the sunrise, and soon the woods were filled with the sound of birds. The bird songs filled the morning air, and Matthews remarked how different some of the sounds were from the bird calls back home.

Matthews' voice pulled John out of his thoughts, "Quite exotic," Matthew said.

"Yes, yes they are." When he heard the song of the first bird, John thought about what Kate Teal might have said on hearing the sound. She'd been so absorbed in the experience of the child on the *Isabella* merely saying the word *bird*; all these most unusual bird calls through the forest would undoubtedly have caused an eruption of conversation from her.

The team dismounted and walked approximately three miles over winding hills and through valleys. The land was more rugged than any they'd seen so far, and since they had 18 miles to go, they tried to keep a good pace. About halfway to Sorocaba, the group came upon 15 or 20 workers repairing the road. This was the first work crew that the scouting team had seen in Brazil, which was a bit of encouragement as improved roads were one of the amenities that the Brazilian government had promised the U.S. citizens if they would relocate. It was one of the incentives for the anticipated increase of agricultural revenue.

The party trudged on, and visibility became more and more limited by a dense fog. They could barely see the second mule and man ahead of them. It was a bit dreary. They were warned to stay strictly on the path. On the highest elevations off to the south and the west, the fog began to rise, making shapes like clouds in the distance.

As the sun came out and began dissipating the fog, majestic rolling valleys were revealed. They were startled by the beauty in which they suddenly became immersed. It was the grandest mountain scenery that John had ever seen. The mountains looked as if they'd been dropped, side by side, leaving deep ravines and hollows in between. When the party was about four miles out of Sorocaba, the mountains became less steep, and the quality of the housing improved. Tiles now replaced thatched roof houses, the land was more level, and the roads were improved.

The party was fatigued from the grueling travel when they checked into a hotel at 3:30 p.m. that proved to be a bit more accommodating than the one in Cotia. Although they were tired, Matthews and Hesse, the interpreter, straightaway delivered letters of introduction to some of the prominent men in the community.

Later that evening, Monarch Sopes D. Olivera and a Mr. Pentacado came to visit with them and offered to show them land for sale. The next morning the group journeyed six miles into the country, had their breakfast which had been packed for them, and spent three hours looking over Pentacado's land. The initial excitement over finding the first cotton patches, even though the plot had been badly cultivated and the yield small, was tempered by the discovery that the harvest-ready bolls were already rotten inside.

Dinner was waiting for the tired and hungry crew when they arrived back at the hotel. The men washed down a hearty meal with Lisbon wine and were refreshed. They discussed the high-quality land they'd seen during the day, as well as the considerable number of ants that they'd observed around the coffee trees.

Four of the mules were proving to be inferior and based on the President's authority they were able to effect a swap. By special invitation, at noon they set out to see Professor Toledo's property.

The professor showed them a gin owned by a Frenchman named Martinas. Martinas had built the gin on Toledo's land and bought cotton from the small farmers in the surrounding countryside. He ginned and baled the cotton, then shipped it to France. The group returned to Toledo's home where they were warmly welcomed by his family and served a good meal, including more Lisbon wine. At dinner, they met a fellow countryman named Robinson from the state of Georgia, a machinist who took care of all of Martinas' engines at the gin. Robinson and the professor encouraged the group, and it was evident they hoped the team would choose their section of the São Paulo region for their new home.

The next morning at about 10, the group set out with the professor in tow to visit a *fazenda* or plantation that was for sale.

However, the owner wasn't at home, so the team moved on. At the next stop, they witnessed an 18-foot saw-gin at work, a small mill for grinding corn, and a machine for pulverizing corn into meal for making *farina*. The machinery was driven by one ox attached to a lever like those used in the States for turning the wheels of cotton gins. The cotton gin press and the mill were both attached to the dwelling. The group had noted early on that in Brazil the machinery always seemed to be very near dwellings, which was unlike the typical layout in the U.S.

The men observed that the lands were better and the ants fewer in the *fazenda* area. They saw another cotton field, poorly planted and cultivated; consequently, the yield was low. The locals didn't seem so discouraged about the poor yield and said they planned to try the following season again. Still, the view of surrounding topography was beautiful with mountains off in the distance between six and 20 miles away. The men enjoyed the evening at the Professor's home as his sons played flute and violin for the crew's entertainment. They were accomplished in their performance, and John learned that Professor Toledo had founded a school of 200 students at one time, but due to lack of prompt payment from the patrons, he'd decided to close the school just months before the arrival of the group.

Toledo presented himself as intelligent and humorous. He didn't speak English, but he understood it reasonably well. The men in John's group observed that It seemed to be a local custom not to include the women of the house in dinners and discussions.

At about 11:30 on July 11 the group set out with Professor Toledo and Mr. Martinas for Tathiery, a *fazenda* about 12 miles away. John felt it was especially helpful to have a local like the professor travel with them. The trip required a considerable amount of concentration and focus on acclimating to each new personality and their level of understanding regarding the mission, as well as the language challenges.

The owner of the place wasn't home when they arrived; but, given the professor's presence, the owner's wife invited them in. About a half hour later, the proprietor came home and welcomed them He was a short, thick-set, black-skinned, black-eyed, black-haired, barefoot Brazilian. The house with its dirt floor had few comforts, but the hospitality of the household was genuine.

Matthews and Toledo took the only bed available; the other four slept on hides on the floor, using their blankets for cover. As he was falling asleep John reflected that he'd never slept in a home of a Black man of any nationality. These were indeed different times. The travelers passed a pleasant evening and just after sunrise had coffee with the family, thanked them for their hospitality, and departed.

Upon leaving his guests, Professor Toledo embraced each of them, another Brazilian custom new to the visitors—men who thought highly of each other embraced upon meeting and departing. John felt that the professor was the perfect example of the adage, "actions speak louder than words." Although the Professor didn't speak English and the scouting team, except for Hesse, the interpreter, didn't speak Portuguese, but by his actions, Toledo made them feel warmly welcomed and kindly entertained.

Over the next day and a half, the team observed the significant diversity of geography. By way of an official letter of introduction, they met Dometrio Leopoldo Macheeds, the epitome of a French gentleman who was also a priest. They passed through very fine *terra roxa* lands and had extensive conversations with three local farmers. This area included the finest lands they'd seen to that point, most of it *terra roxa*, purple in color, and well-timbered virgin forests —the first real forest the group had observed. They also saw cane growing, sometimes as much as 70 feet high. It was the time of year when cane was at its highest. Planters used the cane in place of ropes to tie up their cotton bales.

In Brazil, the bales were formed into packages 30 inches long, and 18 inches wide and thick, each weighing three and a half *arrobas* or around 120 pounds, making it possible to efficiently carry cotton to market on mules either to São Paulo or Santos. The seeds were removed by hand or by some process of rollers and proved to be very tedious. The most serious objection to the land in this area was the scarcity of water. The people of Tathiery all used common seep wells, some of them 100 feet deep.

After traveling about 20 more miles, the group arrived in the village of Pirapora, a village of about 500 inhabitants, John wasn't well and had succumbed to one of the sick headaches he experienced from time to time. He was, again, a bit underwhelmed by their accommodations—a small white-washed house made of mud, stick, and *cipro* perched along the Tiete River.

On Saturday, July 14, a good night's sleep had resolved John's headache, and he was ready with his fellow travelers to set out for Porto Feliz, another 18 miles away. They arrived at about 3 p.m. and were comfortably accommodated by Senhor Custodio De Moracus. De Moracus was overseeing some work being done on various machinery around his gin, the second gin of any size that the group had observed. It was a 40-saw gin worked by a six-horse engine.

At this location, the men saw two acres of tea growing and were told that it produced very well but had mostly been abandoned for the cultivation of cotton. John wasn't sure this was the right decision on the part of the planters as it appeared the cotton would mature in the rainy season and surely be destroyed, but he kept his thoughts to himself and said nothing to their hosts, only sharing such observations later within his group. It was a mystery to John how the patrons, guides, and intercessors would show up at various points along the journey, staying for varying lengths of time, then departing.

In their ramblings, they met a Catholic priest, who again, just as the earlier priest they'd met, treated them very kindly. John was somewhat perplexed by the cultural and racial mix of the folks he was meeting in Brazil. He had witnessed all shades between White, Black, and Indian. The Padre, as the group informally referred to him in familiar Spanish, was copper in color with a muscular frame. He was a happy fellow and seemed to enjoy the company of the Americans genuinely. They were grateful that Mr. Aubertin, the railway manager, had sent letters of introductions for them to this kind gentleman. The Padre traveled with the crew about six miles to a *fazenda* that was offered for sale.

As they arrived late in the day, the group didn't have a lot of time for riding over the property, but they did see stunted sugar cane the color of straw, and the scouting crew later found that the height of the cane wasn't relative to the soil quality, but to the type of cane. The shorter cane, which only grew to three or four feet tall, produced a type of juice which required less boiling before it granulated than the taller cane. The rows were narrow at two feet apart and only one foot between each planting. The Padre said that from a distance, the mature cane looked like a solid mass. He also reported the yield from this type of cane was equivalent to the best lands in Louisiana. The price of the *fazenda* was two to three dollars per acre. The Padre knew the Americans had been told that the cost of the land near the city might be cheaper, and he was quick to add that should they purchase land in the vicinity he'd personally ensure that a church of their denomination would be established.

At Porto Feliz, the crew enjoyed warm greetings from Brazilians from the rural areas who expressed that they hoped the Americans would settle among them. Since the itinerary provided the opportunity to remain a little longer at Porto Feliz, John was able to build two model plows for Senhor Morceaus and the Padre, who seemed very pleased and anxious to learn how they worked.

While John finished the fabrication of the plows, Joe Matthews began to explain, through the interpreter, how the equipment worked and how much manual labor would be saved. His explanation was quite lengthy, but neither John nor Mr. Matthews was sure that they understood enough of the explanation to put the plows to practical use. The cotton on this plantation hadn't grown well during the current year, but Morceaus indicated that he'd give it another try next year. If he had rot again next year, he said he'd seriously reconsider trying to grow the crop at the current location.

The next day, three of the Padre's friends joined the party for the trek to Iter. Some of the lands on this side of Porto Feliz appeared to be good land, but after only a few miles it became poorer and more mountainous again and continued this way all the way into Iter.

However, Iter, itself, was a pretty town with street grids familiar to John, which of course, gave him comfort. Some of the houses were two-story residences and were built partly of very fine rosewood, which, if polished, John thought would shine like fine furniture. The main crop of cultivation for this host family was coffee. Coffee required a higher elevation for growing than did most crops and the high fertile lands sold for $40 per acre while the land in the valley sold for two and three dollars, or even less per acre as it was only good for pasture land.

Once again, the group found the ants to be a troublesome affair for the landowners. The plantation manager explained that a half-dozen workers were required to control the ant population on a plantation of 100 workers. These workers dedicated themselves to destroying the ants wherever and whenever they made an appearance. The gentlemen continued their discussion for a couple of hours after dinner, then retired.

The group set out at 8 a.m. for an introduction to the Barra of Piracicada, who was an older gentleman, maybe 75 or 80 years old. They found him perched on a stool in the orchard, engaged in conversation about the fruit with workers. John marveled at the fine orchard of 100 acres or more teeming with orange, peach, lemon, and apple trees, pineapple plants, ornamental trees, and vines. He remarked that the sight was just about the most beautiful agricultural plot he'd ever seen.

"Matthews, I wager there's $10,000 worth of orange trees here."

"You may be right, John, but the old man is worried about them. Blight has set in, and he's trying to determine how to curb it before he loses the whole lot of them. He said over 1,000 trees are already affected by the disease. Notice the oranges on the ground, rotting. There's not enough market in the small town of Iter to absorb them, and it's too far to get them back over to São Paulo or Santos for sale."

At the outer edges of the orchard an unknown species of pine had been planted, some of which were 20 inches in diameter and 60 feet tall. The trees were dense like a forest but planted in rows. However, the fruit trees were the main preoccupation of the Barra, so the scouts garnered little information about the pines.

After walking the orchard for an hour or so, the party returned to the Barra's home where they were treated to breakfast and coffee. For the first time in their journey, the woman of the house served the coffee to the Americans. John felt this added an air of civilization he'd sorely missed. He enjoyed the company of women of all kinds.

After breakfast, the Barra and six of his countrymen rode with the scouting party to the waterfall on the Tiete River. The ledge that created the fall was about 20 feet high. The Barra explained that many fine fish inhabited the river. John was always interested in the machinery of the locale, and at the waterfall, he spied an 18-saw gin at work, not unlike the one they'd experienced a few days earlier, but certainly much smaller than the 50-saw gin he'd observed in Iter. He noticed that neither of the gins seemed to work especially efficiently and he surmised that their uselessness was relative to the size of the bands used in propelling them. They were too small to get sufficient power to run them with velocity enough to make a good full tight roll; consequently, the seeds fell from the saw before they were properly cleaned. John was confident that he could make the adjustments needed, but their schedule didn't permit time for his efforts.

By dark, they'd arrived at Capivary, a small town situated on a river bank. The town had less than 500 inhabitants, and the accommodations were poor, but after the long ride of the day, the group slept well and continued traveling the next morning for the *fazenda* of Monte Attenlegro. At the outset, the land was poor, but after six miles they began to see fine, verdant timber and plantation spreads.

At about 3:30 p.m., they arrived at their destination and were greeted by Senhor Cartas Ponto, a member of the Brazilian congress, who warmly welcomed the group and offered refreshments. Dinner was a fine festive affair as they dined with Senhor Ponto's wife, the Marquezan of Monte Attenlegro, and Ponto's two daughters by his former marriage. John figured the Marquezan was about 40 years old and wasn't an attractive woman, but polite. Her house was well kept, and she served a good table. Senhor Ponto's was accommodating as well.

Based on minimal evidence, John thought that the marriage was probably one of convenience. Rumor had it that Ponto had married the older woman for her money. Her first husband, the Marquez, was said to have been a rich old fool who married the woman when she wasn't much more than a girl. He died a few years later, leaving all his property to her, and years later, Cartas Ponto married her.

John's desire to explain a better way of farming got the best of him. John observed that the plows were rudely constructed and threw up large clods of dirt and rough cultivated patches. As the party had more time the day of their visit to Ponto's place, he fabricated a model plow and did his best to explain how it worked to the Senhor. John wasn't sure how much was lost in the translation or how much the gentleman was able to comprehend, but he felt better for having offered a better solution. Surely, Ponto would figure it out.

That evening was the most entertaining they'd experienced on the journey. The men had been summoned to an early supper at about 4 p.m. The Marquezan had prepared a dinner worthy of any celebration with meats, vegetables, fruits, and pastries arranged tantalizingly on serving platters; and the conversation was light and engaging, John thought about some of the wonderful holiday and Sunday dinner meals that had been served at his table in the past. Cynthia was an excellent cook, and she'd taught their daughters, and their neighbors' daughters as well, the art of well-seasoned greens and cobblers brimming over with fresh peaches or blackberries and cream. She could also make a fine coconut cake.

As he passed the serving dish of fresh fruits from Ponto's orchard, he found his thoughts shifting to Kate Teal and realized he looked forward to telling her about his journey. He knew she'd marvel at the orchard and probably would've wanted to stay longer there than the party had time for.

After dinner, Joe and John walked about the *fazenda* grounds. Ponto had fine hogs and imported cows. As the sun set, a Catholic Priest from Piracicaba region joined them when they went inside for tea. The Marquezan had brought out a variety of puzzles and games of sorts to help entertain the visitors.

John was happy about the diversion. Trying to keep a conversation going with the language barriers was a real chore. He'd complained to Matthews that sometimes he felt they were a group of monkeys on exhibition. The language barrier had wearied John. He promised himself that if he ever traveled to a foreign country again, he'd learn at least the rudimentary elements of their language first. He had found it tiresome to try to get and give information through an interpreter; and, due to the various local idioms, he wasn't always sure the translation was reliable. It had been difficult to find interpreters who understood both the Portuguese and the southern English well enough. The technical details, such as the discussion around the gins, were added problems.

The next morning Ponto accompanied them to the river Piracicaba where they fashioned a float by fastening two canoes together and ported their provisions across. When they arrived at Moro Azul, they went straight to the home of Senhor Antonio Silverai Joedairo and were immediately invited to dinner, after which they toured his property.

John was duly impressed. He thought the farm was the most beautiful farm he'd ever seen. Joedairo had 386,000 coffee trees and planned to plant 150,000 more. At this point, all the trees seemed healthy and well. He anticipated that his 200 slaves would gather 3,000 *arrobas*, the equivalent to 96,000 pounds of beans in the coming year. Joedairo appeared very methodical and organized in his management practices, which John appreciated.

Joedairo invited the guests to breakfast then rode with them far enough to put them on the right road to Commander Nicolau Jose de Campos Vergueiro's *fazenda*. They arrived in short order and were met, much to their delight, by Colonel Adams of Alabama. Adams had been awaiting them for some time. Two weeks before their arrival John had sent a brief letter alerting him that they were in the vicinity. Since the Commander was away from the *fazenda*, his foreman Angelico did the honors of welcoming the scouting party and showing them around the place.

Vergueiro farmed on a grand scale. The visiting party learned that he was the largest planter in the province with 1,500,000 coffee trees and planned to obtain another 500,000. Adams was in the employ of Vergueiro, coordinating the manufacture of plows, which John was thrilled to learn, and he also led what was referred to on the *fazenda* as "the cotton experiment."

The previous year Vergueiro had planted 400 acres of cotton, which didn't do very well, but in the current year, he had planned for 3,000 more acres. Vergueiro was not easily discouraged. Coffee had been his only crop the previous year. Eight hundred slaves worked the *fazendo*, and they were expected to harvest 120,000 *arrobas* of coffee that year. The harvest was considered a rather small yield, but not disappointing to Vergara.

Vergueiro himself arrived at about 7 p.m. He was an interesting study of a man—medium build, middle-aged with a distinguished amount of gray hair and gray whiskers. John thought he looked very much like a German, except his complexion was rather dark. His fast manner of speaking seemed to be an outcome of his nervous energy. John learned that his initial perception of Vergueiro wasn't far off the mark, Vergueiro had lived in Germany for several years and was educated there. He seemed perfectly comfortable speaking the German language and spoke English very well, although he often relied on Adams to articulate his views and feelings. John felt Vergueiro was coarse and that his manners lacked warmth, which he attributed to the fact that he had served as an officer in the German army.

However little he cared for him, John had to acknowledge the fact that his agriculture was the most advanced that the group had seen. While they were observing the farm, Adams put a half-dozen plows to work for demonstration purposes. Although Adams had overseen the demonstration from the making of the plow to the plowing, John wasn't impressed with the workings, beginning with the harnessing of the mules. The spacing between the machines and animals was too significant.

During their three days at Jose Vergueiro's *fazenda*, John learned that Vergueiro's wife was also his first cousin. She spoke no English, and consequently, there was little dialogue between her and the visitors. She appeared intelligent and accomplished. Adams relayed that he held her in the highest esteem, saying that she was as kind to him as a sister would be and a perfect model of a wife. John watched her as she moved across the dining room, the parlor, the veranda. He felt she knew he watched her, but she acknowledged him only twice with a brief warm smile.

The visit to the Vergueiro *fazenda* had been educational as the Americans knew little to nothing about growing and cultivating coffee. They had observed that the coffee beans were first gathered from the trees and poured into vats with enough water to cover them, allowing them to set for 24 hours. The water was then allowed to drain off, and the beans were carried to a machine which separated the outside hull from the bean kernel. After being separated from the hulls, the beans fell into a large flat basin into which water ran continuously. At this juncture, the beans were raked and stirred until they were well washed. Finally, they were washed out of the vat by opening a lever into a small ditch lined with brick.

The ditch was about two feet wide and two feet deep with a slight fall at intervals of 10 feet or so. The coffee beans, which were carried by water along the ditch, could be stopped at any of the intervals for inspection and culling. The smaller and more imperfect grains were separated from the first quality at the end of the ditch, then the prime product was carried to larger flumes, made of bricks that were about six inches thick, to dry. After they dried sufficiently, they were then carried to a machine that knocked off the inner hull and part of the skin immediately upon the grain.

At the same time, a fan separated the chaff from the beans which moved down through screens separating the different size beans. As the beans fell from the machine, Negro slave women and girls gathered them up, shook and sifted them through more wire screens, all the while, picking out any defective beans which may have escaped the machine further up the line. Lastly, the beans were put into sacks for transportation. Using this production line that the German described was said to have cut the processing time down from 40 days to 10.

The group was impressed by the amount of machinery at Vergueiro's fazenda—a foundry for metal work, a sawmill and grist mills, lathes, and carpenter bricks. Vergara had trained foremen sufficiently for each task. He had two clerks that assigned the work to be done each day. It was said that Vergueiro, himself, began his work at 4 a.m. each day and was busy all day experimenting with some piece of work or machinery around the coffee mill or gins. Adams had shared a story of how Vergara had his screws organized by the shape of head and size of the thread, an effort John thought was maybe one step too much.

Vergueiro's beloved *fazenda*, *Yibicaba*, had approximately 90 German families living on it, some of the men were employed as mechanics and machinists; women gathered the coffee and were said to be fine workers, but their pay was barely their subsistence.

There were some issues with translation, but Vergueiro seemed to think having the German families on his plantation to work was a kind gesture on his part.

He was very interested in seeing Americans settle in the immediate area and offered to sell them any of his land outside the *Yibicaba* at a third of its valuation, with 100 slaves to help get the new place started.

John took the evening to write a letter to Cynthia and share that he hoped she was keeping an open mind. While he wasn't sure yet, he'd heard of and seen, first-hand, some encouraging opportunities in the territory south of São Paulo, Brazil. He focused on the support the scouts received in each community they visited and on the warm welcome they'd received from area planters. The fact that there was a certain amount of machinery in place and for those planters needing slave labor, slaves seemed abundantly available.

He shared with her that he understood if they could get a group of 10 to 20 families together to purchase land and form a community by building their own church, calling a preacher and establishing a school that they could govern themselves, somewhat as they chose, with certain municipal privileges granted by the larger government.

John asked about Cynthia's well-being, as well as that of his daughters and neighbors. He asked Cynthia to write to him and told her they would hold his mail at the Hotel Europa in São Paulo. He didn't mention that when it came to establishing a school, he might have already met a woman who could handle that task.

He signed the letter, "With deep and abiding love, John." John enlisted the foreman Angelico, who had already proved to be very helpful, to help with getting the letter into the mail going back to Alabama.

The scouting party didn't see the farm at Angelseo that Vergueiro offered, but he and Adams said it was indeed fine land and could be sectioned into large parcels. The group was also told that beyond this area, approximately 24 miles from Rio Clero, there was a beautiful country with soil as rich as could be seen anywhere. These lands were owned by people who were a mixture of Indian, Negro, and White. They were called *Cabodo* and were described as a wilder set of people, but there appeared to be some level of awareness that these folks would be willing to sell their land.

Col. William Hutchinson Norris, who was a lawyer and had been a senator in Alabama, met the party at Vergueiro's *fazenda* and traveled with them to his own place. Over the next 25 miles or so they passed the attractive little village of Limeira, which John estimated had 800 inhabitants, at the most. In this region, they passed several small coffee farms and small cotton farms as well.

During the War Between the States, the entire world, no place more than England, was speculating on where cotton production would shift. The British were financing farmers in Egypt, India, and Brazil.

Mr. Aubertine, an Englishman who was also the manager of the southern part of the Brazilian railway, was enticed by the Manchester Association to try to encourage the Brazilians to cultivate cotton. His effort initially met with success as cotton was easier to cultivate compared to coffee, and the high price of cotton made it seem worth the risk for small farmers to undertake the new effort.

The Brazilians took to the new crop quickly and had produced good yields. For a period, the whole of Brazil had gone a bit crazy about the subject of cotton, or *algodão*. However, the weather in the last season hadn't been conducive to cotton growing, and many small farms experienced crop failure. If the cotton price dropped as it was anticipated, John presumed that many of the small farmers would be so discouraged that they would abandon the idea of growing cotton.

It was about 5 p.m. when they arrived at Colonel Norris' place where the colonel immediately introduced the group to his son Robert, who was living on the *fazenda* and attempting to grow cotton using hired hands. Robert had an upbeat temperament and they all enjoyed his company, as a spirit of optimism was an ever-present need in a strange company.

The property adjacent to Norris's was in flux. A Mr. Cole, from Mississippi, had put the land under initial contract before he left for his return visit to Mississippi to get his family and others who were relying on his effort to find a new home for them in Brazil. Cole left the final details of the land purchase with an agent, a Mr. Griffith who had served as a Confederate soldier. By further investigation Griffith found that the title to the land wasn't clear; consequently, he didn't finalize the purchase, and it remained unsettled as to whether Mr. Norris would have Mr. Cole as a neighbor.

The next day, the group rode over portions of Norris's property. He seemed settled in the new country and had considerable plans, including rebuilding his residence in a slightly different location and in a more traditional manner. The house in which he currently resided was made of mud and upright posts, not suitable for the property owner.

On the *fazenda*, Norris had established a well, from which the water was cool, refreshing, and had a good taste. He had a grist mill and small sawmill, all run by water and located within 50 yards of the current residence. The lead on the water to run the machinery was collected more than a half mile from the residence and was fed from a branch of the Quilombo River, just out of their sight. Nearby there was a large pond filled with fine fish and with, as the story was told, an alligator or two.

Robert was having phenomenal success growing a watermelon, the seeds of which they'd brought to Brazil. The Georgia Rattlesnake, as it was called, was at the very end of its growing season. Young fellas working nearby found a couple of stragglers and dropped them in the branch to cool them, so the scouting party could enjoy a taste before moving on. The thought of a sweet, juicy, red watermelon gave John one more point of familiarity to add to his list.

John observed a variety of bees, and when he questioned Robert Norris, he found him to be quite expert on the subject. One variety was similar in size to the ones that John had experienced back home. He had also witnessed a larger bee and a honey bee that made a honey that young Norris told John had medicinal purposes.

The bees were said to make no more than a gallon and a half of honey per hive. John had also seen wasps, a variety that was said to infest the hollows of trees and swarm in ordinary seasons attacking both animals and people. The Colonel said the locals had a holy horror of these wasps and when they saw them swarming, they stopped what they were doing and took cover. Robert shared that there hadn't been any attacks by the swarming wasps in years because the insects' food supply had been abundant lately.

Norris and his son accompanied the party for four miles as they rode towards Campinas, which was about 18 miles away. Norris seemed at a genuine loss when it was time to say goodbye. It was evident that he, like Senhor Vergueiro a few days before, had hoped some faction of these scouts would be new American settlers in the region. John heard the Colonel clearly when he spoke of gathering enough expatriates together to form an independent community.

As they crossed the edge of the bordering Machadinho Estate and neared the town, they saw coffee farms once again dotting the landscape. John surmised that the value of the land would increase with the promise of the railroad being extended to Campinas from Jundia, where it presently terminated.

For the first time since the expedition began, the scouting party discovered many of their letters of introduction to landowners in Campinas to be of little use, as many of the proprietors weren't to be found. The nephew of Senhor Ivaguere Amoral's happily escorted the group about five miles out of town to introduce them to Mr. Morrison from Missouri, who ran a blacksmith station of sorts.

Old man Morrison made plows of the old *dagon* style were used in Alabama 15 or 20 years before. The plow was a swing plow variation which needed no wheels and had no foot for support on the end of the beam. The men were polite, but no one was overly impressed by the old man's work. The visitors strolled on to a house where they understood they could refresh themselves with water and rest a bit. To their surprise, they were invited for beer and wine and to a full dinner attended by the women of the family.

The women were generous with servings and with their smiles. The guests and host made conversation the best they could, looked at the coffee machinery on the place, and then headed back to town. They rode through small coffee plantations that appeared to run the full gamut in appearance from quite orderly to much less so, even disorderly. From what the Americans understood, the planters could expect only two to three pounds of coffee as the average yield from each tree.

The party's next stop was Jundia, about 18 miles from Campinas. The ride was arduous, and when the team arrived, they felt fatigued, had a quick dinner, and went to bed. The men discussed taking the train back to São Paulo but couldn't understand clearly enough to be comfortable with the answer regarding precisely when the next train would arrive. Consequently, they all agreed to stay the course and ride their horses on to São Paulo, 33 miles away.

The terrain was mountainous, but even John had to admit that the road was in pretty good condition; it was the best road they'd traveled on during their expedition. John believed a fully stocked wagon would be able to pass over the road for the full duration of the journey. On other roads, he'd observed poor construction and other obstacles that would've made it nearly impossible for wagons to maintain an acceptable pace. They had been fine for mule and horseback, but not especially suitable for wagons. After about 20 miles, the scouts decided to rest in a little place called Peru.

Early the next morning, which was the last day of July, they headed out with the intention of being back in the city by midday. The gentlemen agreed to meet again in the hotel lobby after they'd taken a few hours to wash up and rest a bit. John took a much-needed nap and being habitually early, was still the first to reach the lobby.

As they waited, his traveling companions joined him one by one. He found that he was distracted by every person who was entering and exiting the building. John realized that he was hoping to catch a glimpse of Kate. He had sent a brief note to Kate by way of the kindness of Robert Norris but had no idea if she'd received it and if she had, what she'd thought of it. The letter had been somewhat of an apology for the kiss. He wasn't sorry for having kissed her, but he didn't want her to feel that he'd been disrespectful in any way. She hadn't seemed offended, but the distance of time and space had caused him to second-guess the encounter.

Settling In

To become more familiar with the community, Kate decided to take a carriage across the neighborhood to the other side of the city where she'd heard there was a bigger market. She felt ready to venture out and begin the negotiations of communication. The small white carriage with large spoked wheels pulled up so close it nearly brushed her skirt. The driver was a dark-skinned man. She didn't know what ethnicity he was. She wasn't yet capable of distinguishing all the shades of humanity that she encountered each day. And, she was less of an oddity than she felt, given the international swirl of this country. Kate found the city's mix of ethnicities both interesting and sometimes a little confusing. She wouldn't have been unhappy if Notch had stayed close by a little longer than he had.

She met the driver's wide smile with one of her own. He took her hand, and she lifted herself, right foot first, into the carriage. She chose to face forward and settled herself on a red leather seat near the left side so that she could see the street ahead.

It was a misty morning, and she felt as if she'd stepped into a scene that might have been painted by the rising French artist Claude Monet. This misty morning gave her a newfound appreciation for his art. The colors of the houses that were typically bright and lively in the sun were muted. Shades of peach melded into a subdued slate blue, and canary yellow wrapped around turquoise like a soft blanket. Sweet potato vines and dark green ivy trailed off balconies, shoring up basket after basket that held white and pink petunias and puffs of red and coral geraniums.

Kate had immediately fallen in love with the colors of this new country. She marveled at how they blended house to house, shop to lean-to, and back again to create pathways that were filled with ordinary people doing ordinary things day after day. It was perhaps the proximity of humanity that made life seem so intense in the city, but it was nonetheless a miracle to Kate that for all its busyness, daily life refused to take itself too seriously. Front yards were fenced, or not, with wrought iron, and some held heavy gates. In other places, the fencing was as much decoration as functional. She loved the way the crepe myrtles grew thick and strong, stretching their twisted trunks to hold the bright bonnet of blooms in assorted tones of purple that shaded the sidewalks. The harder rain that had fallen at daybreak had caused puddles of blooms all along the way. It was the stuff of fairy tales she thought—purple rain. As Kate tilted her head to see further down a side alley, she caught the sound of the bells jingling on the wide neck of the *regal mula branca* that pulled the carriage. His hooves gently made a rhythmic clopping along the brick street. There was absolutely nothing to do but absorb this moment of color and sound and fresh rain. She stopped worrying about whether she could make a good deal at the market or what tomorrow might bring. Kate became aware of her breathing and felt herself exhale into this Thursday morning canvas—a very special day and yet one that had happened over and over for hundreds of years whether anyone noticed or not.

Although she'd only taught for a short period before she was married, Kate was hoping that her education for teaching would be worth something in her new life.

Her first order of business was to purchase a new book of Portuguese and English translations. She had a slight book with only the most basic of phrases that she'd bought when she and Notch were in Baltimore. As neither of them knew any Portuguese, they found trying to decipher the pronunciations was more than awkward; however, they'd found some help from one of the *Isabella's* Spanish crewmen, who knew as much English as Portuguese, and they began learning the new language.

She found most of the shopkeepers, tailors, and cafe workers to be patient with her struggles with the language. Generally, in a matter of minutes, she could convey her needs. The language tumbled off the tongues of patriots like a rapid rush of water spilling over the edge of a crevice. It all ran together in her hearing. Recognizing written words was easier for her than understanding the spoken word, so there was a good bit of printing words and picture drawing that resembled impromptu games of charades. Basic communication was an adventure.

She ventured out mostly in the mid-mornings. She was mindful in her outings to bring some food back to her room to replace eating in the hotel restaurant. Usually, her provisions included fruit, more than she was used to consuming, and bread or pastry. Her favorites were the sweet oranges and *abacaxi* or pineapple, but she found them difficult to cut in her room. Like the locals, she chose the *abacaxi,* along with *mamao* or *papaia*, for breakfast, She found the *carambola* the most interesting with its ribbed edges. The star shape amused her when she sliced it horizontally. It made when she sliced it horizontally. She learned to like the *acai* berries which were brought in from the Amazon region. The berries were a purplish black and reminded Kate of large blueberries back home. Tea was inexpensive and easy to come by in the hotel.

Within a few days, she was able to find a reasonable room at a boarding house not too far from the Presbyterian mission. Kate was delighted to meet Reverend Robert Powers and his wife Anna Catherine Arnold Powers, missionaries from America, who were interested in starting an American school. They had already begun to hold classes in their home.

As Kate shared her educational background with the Powers, she was pleased that they were already aware of the excellent education that the Tennessee and Alabama Female Institute offered women. It was the first women's college to offer equivalent degrees to those provided by men's colleges, including advanced mathematics, Latin and Greek, grammar and composition, philosophy, geography, and geology, as well as botany, chemistry, astronomy, and physiology. It was a radical curriculum for women patterned after those offered at Amherst College, Brown University and the University of Virginia. The school's roots were in the Baptist Church, but its academic reach was phenomenal. Kate had been engrossed in getting a broad-based education and enjoyed the time she'd spent in the foothills of Appalachia.

Even though Kate was an Episcopalian by declaration, she was comfortable with the Powers, and on many Sundays, she attended the mission church. Sharing tea with the couple was part of her

Thursday afternoon siesta. Kate enjoyed being immersed in the expansive thinking of her new friends. Their plans for establishing a school were revolutionary by Brazilian standards and by American standards that Kate had witnessed.

The Powers were steadfast in their plan to develop an educational opportunity that included no corporal punishment and attendance of both genders in the same classes, but beyond these precepts, Kate was inspired by the openness to students from all ethnic backgrounds, social classes, and religious denominations. They were by far the most enlightened people that Kate had the opportunity to get to know on a personal level. Their inclusive spirit deeply attracted her. They, in turn, were impressed with Kate's formal education, aptitude for openness to educational theories and appreciation for the fact that learned belief systems are at the basis of how individuals interpret the world. She understood immediately that building a culture of openness and tolerance for diverse opinion was at the heart of creating a more progressive society.

Kate realized that the Powers were establishing an opportunity for educating students that was beyond her wildest dreams, which were to work primarily with children of American immigrants. Working with the Powers would help her to grow intellectually, as well as, spiritually, at an accelerated rate. As the Powers' vision became more tangible with classes for elementary school-aged children outgrowing the space in their home, they were able to include Kate as their first paid teaching staff.

Since funding for the school was still such a challenge, Anna Catherine offered Kate living space in a small cabin set at the back of the mission property in which an old grounds caretaker had lived before his recent death. The cabin needed an industrious tenant to improve its condition. While Kate wasn't very skilled at carpentry, she knew a good cleaning, paint, curtains, and a couple of area rugs would go a long way toward sprucing up the place. Kate agreed and immediately began planning the work for which she did excel — gardening vegetables, flowers, and herbs.

Kate loved reading and journaling in her new peaceful environment. She didn't know how long she'd been sitting, wrapped in her shawl, watching the first light fall across the still dense and variegated green that comes with the winter rain. She noticed the movement of a solitary leaf hanging on the bottom of a rusty forgotten birdcage, propped on a stump near the corner of the *casa pequena*. There was no wind current. A breeze didn't cause the movement. She looked closer to be sure that she'd not imagined the movement. She found her observation true to the moment. A small brown dried rosewood leaf hung tenuously from the cage bottom and wiggled, not by the power of the wind, but by the power of some tiny thing encapsulated. The movement was subtle, at times hardly noticeable, then fierce like a cat fighting its way out of a Crocker sack. She wasn't knowledgeable enough with entomology to know what kind of insect might be fighting its way out of the closed dark space, but she had great empathy for it as the struggle in the tacky filament seemed to parallel the feeling she carried around in her head these days—the belief that some idea, some answer was trying to manifest itself, but couldn't quite make its way to consciousness.

She'd been sleeping too long, shut down by the alternate chaos and the nothingness that had surrounded her for the last several years in America. Maybe they were the same. Chaos was the result of no resolution. Finding resolution had been as empty and futile as the empty stares of unknowing that sat around kitchen tables, filled local businesses, and other public places.

The energy inside the leaf enthralled her. How could something so tiny be so persistent in moving toward the light? What would its chances of survival be? Why was it so driven to break from its hiding place? It was a change of life calling, a call that couldn't be resisted, even if it required every ounce of energy to create the change. Her eyes grew heavy as she focused intently on this one spot. She was afraid to divert her attention for fear of whatever was inside flying or crawling away and her missing the first expression of this new life outside the cocoon. In all the world, the garden was her favorite place to be. As she sipped her *chá preto quente*, as she had learned to call hot tea, she felt the warm morning sun on her face and breathed in the scent of lavender which fortified her for the rest of the day.

Death Is Not the End

Kate closed the book of contemporary poetry after reading the brief but weighty poem by Emily Dickinson of Massachusetts. It began, 'I heard a fly buzz—when I died—' and ended 'And then the Windows failed—and then I couldn't see to see–.' How appropriate she thought.

This was the day they had buried Margaret, a friend Kate had made while doing small maintenance tasks around the church. For the sake of entertaining themselves, Margaret and Kate put a list of topics in a crystal bowl and on Sunday morning each drew a topic for the week. They wrote whatever and however, they chose on the topic. The writing could be poetry, could be an essay, could be humorous, could be serious. Then they shared. In the sharing, the other person was to write a response to the first person's reaction to the topic. They had been at this endeavor for weeks and enjoyed each other's weekly company mid-afternoon on Thursdays when they shared their responses after they excused themselves from enjoying *chá preto quente* with the Powers.

Margaret was at least two dozen year's Kate senior and seemingly in good health. When the groundskeeper of the church, Afonso, brought Kate the news, he merely said "Poor Ms. Margaret, *Coração parou de bater.*" Margaret had come to Brazil many years earlier as part of the group from Virginia that was helping to get Episcopal churches started in Brazil. Her husband died in an accident near Santos during a construction project, and she chose to remain in São Paulo, a city they'd grown to love.

Kate found her to be not only extremely intelligent and feisty, but interesting and empathetic, as well, and she cherished their friendship. Her husband was buried adjacent to the church's larger cemetery because non-Brazilians were not allowed to be buried directly in the cemetery. Kate assumed that Margaret would be buried by his side.

Margaret's friend Frederica came by to ask Kate for some of Margaret's writings to share as part of the eulogy. Kate smiled to herself at the request. Because the two had done most of their writing in the shadow of the church's steeple, Margaret had said she wanted to be buried in the sound of her own words; her voice left behind for whoever was there to hear it. She and Margaret had a good laugh about her comment that day, and now, it seemed to Kate a pleasant premonition, although Margaret was joking at the time. Kate saved everything she and her friend had written in their exchange together and pulled out a few of the ruminations for Frederica.

As Kate took her time climbing the multi-leveled steps leading to the church, her heart heavy and a knot in her throat, she thought, "So here you are Margaret, being buried today in the sound of your own voice; impacting me as much as ever. No dying is not the end, is it, my friend?

Exploration Continues

When the core group, including Dr. Punto and Mr. Hesse, the interpreter, arrived back in São Paulo, they shared a wonderful dinner and then set out to thank the president of the province for his support of their highly informative journey. Much to the group's surprise, the president again provided financial support of $650 for their excursion to Cananéia and Iguape. To allow time to restock supplies and frankly to rest a bit, the men decided they'd spend a few days in town and pick up the next excursion in about a week's time.

Joe Matthews, Dan Hall, and John spent the first day of August touring São Paulo. John was duly impressed by the vista behind the president's palace. The trekkers were surprised by a herd of steers bound for an exhibition in Rio. The cattle were first to be moved to Santos, then by water to Rio. The steers were full grown but not fattened according to the standards in the U.S. Some of them were as much as five feet high and had very long horns. The fellas picked out one animal they estimated to be six feet from point to point.

Subsequently, John and his clan were off to see a brickyard located just a couple of miles from town. The yard was modern with machinery from H. Clayton & Company Patenters and Makers of London. John immediately recognized that the bricks produced in this yard were the same bricks he'd seen in some of the public buildings, including the market house in São Paulo. At the brickyard, he was able to see that the peculiar distinction of the brick was caused by holes made through the center of the bricks. Incorporating these holes created a curing process that used less fire and shorter drying times, making construction more economical.

Feeling more like a tourist than a scout now, John spent the week visiting additional locations that he wouldn't have if the time had been more restrictive. He climbed up a church steeple where he had a broad view of the city and found it very pleasing.

John Foster, Punto, Hall, Matthews, and Carlos regrouped and made it to Santos by 5 p.m. where they checked into Hotel Viajantes. Whenever John was alone, his thoughts would drift to Kate Teal. How was she managing? Was she still in this area? Did she receive his letter? Had she found a school or employment? Was she glad that she'd made the trip or was she reconsidering her options? Where was she?

John spent most of the next day walking around the city and catching up in his scouting journal. Later that evening, Matthews, Hall, and John made their way to the residence of a Mr. Wright, who welcomed them into his home for dinner. The gentlemen were introduced to Mrs. Wright, who appeared to be, at least in part, of Spanish descent. It was apparent that English wasn't her first language, but she did speak it well, as did the Wright's three daughters. Mrs. Wright seemed genuinely happy to have the company and saw to it that all were engaged in polite conversation. After a while, she played the piano while Mr. Wright accompanied her, from time to time, singing songs that were familiar to them and pleasant to the visitors' ear as well.

As he had no routine, John found that it was easy to lose track of the days of the week, especially with no church services. He missed the fellowship of his church family back home, but he reminded himself that nothing had been routine since the fighting broke out, and the preachers were called out in every direction to minister to all sorts of needs.

Measuring time was mostly left to the natural occurrences of sunrise and sunset rather than an agenda of tasks and work. On this Sunday morning, Foster, Hall, and Matthews joined Dr. Punto again, along with two Spanish consuls and a few other gentlemen aboard a small steamer for a tour of a 16-mile inlet, after which they disembarked and walked two miles to the *fazenda* of Senhor Valendor Leonel. The Leonel *fazenda* was situated on the beach which John found delightful. The party walked along the beach, which was just some 200 yards from the house. The gardens and the juxtaposition of the house to the ocean reminded John of Beauvoir, the coastal home of widow Dorsey.

For the second time that day, John found himself homesick. About a half mile down the beach Senhor Leonel showed his guests his prime fishing ground. The group pulled traps that had previously been set and returned to Leonel's to prepare a very nice mess of fish for their dinner. After dinner, they returned to the beach. John was impressed with its beauty and the lack of impediments, which made it ideal for swimming.

The men pulled more traps and found plentiful fish, including the curious Devil Fish and Sword Fish. Leonel told the men that the fishing was so excellent that it provided a significant amount of income for the *fazenda*, approximately $500 per month in the high season. He explained that there was some processing involved with selling the fish, as they were dried first and put in small boxes or casks. Having stayed longer than anticipated enjoying the beach and information provided by Senhor Leonel, the group was pleased when Leonel further extended his hospitality and invited them to stay on for the night. Although they hadn't planned to do so, given the hour, they agreed. The large crowd of 12 or so spread out through the house and around the grounds for their respite.

After drinking a quick morning cup of coffee, the pack was off, first by canoe, then by steamer back to Santos. Aboard the steamer, they ate cold meats and cheese to hold them over and arrived back in the city at 11 a.m. The men rested for the remainder of the day and joined the Wright household again in the early evening for tea.

On August 7th, the explorers began a very different part of their excursion as they left Santos for Iguape on a large canoe paddled by four men. At about the 11-mile mark, they arrived at the *fazenda* of Antonio deSilva. They docked and unloaded provisions they'd brought along for deSilva. The family seemed genuinely happy to have the visitors.

Mrs. deSilva prepared the dinner table, complete with forks and knives. She served sumptuous platters of roasted oysters. John blurted out, "Senhor deSilva, why these are the finest oysters I think I've ever seen and with them, I mark a birthday that I'll never forget!" The deSilva family and John's new friends cheered and toasted John Bailey Foster's 15th birthday. Antonio deSilva helped his wife explain the preparation process to John. The oyster shells were washed off and then placed on a grate over hot coals of an open fire where they were heated until the shells popped open. The flavor of the oysters was enhanced by the scant sprinkling of a local pepper sauce.

The crew left the *fazenda* about 5 p.m., and after about two and a half hours more of rowing ended up at the end of the stream. Then they trod across a sandy road in the dark for two miles until they reached another sea beach. At this point, they were provided with wagons, more like carts, which were to be drawn by oxen. Each cart was covered by rushes and rawhide to make it waterproof. Two to a cart, they climbed in and found that they had to position themselves in somewhat of a reclining position with legs stretched out as they couldn't manage to sit up straight due to the limited height of the makeshift covering. They experienced an odd sensation as they journeyed across the sea beach with the tide sometimes passing under the carts while the oxen trudged on.

"Boys that trek last night was an interesting ride! At one point, I woke up and was sure our driver had deserted us and left the oxen to pull us into the ocean. I could hear the water rushing under us and almost feel the cart afloat!" John was the most likely of the bunch to say what he was thinking, sometimes to the group's mild remorse, but they all laughed at his comment, and the driver assured them that all was well.

The trek along the beach was a slow 32 miles, with the crew arriving at Cananéia at 9 a.m., eating breakfast by 11, after which they were again herded into carts, two men in each, pulled by two mules that were guided by a driver. The driver walked behind the carts, focusing attention to one side of the cart then the other and guiding the animals by a sharp rap of the pole.

They traveled in this miserable fashion until almost midnight when they arrived at Peruibe, their destination. They were given dinner, and each was provided with a mat and shown a space where they could sleep on the floor in a dark room. In the morning light, they found the village of Peruibe to be a settlement of about 12 houses in various stages of disrepair. John felt a little sorry for the dirty, ragged children that ran about.

After a simple breakfast, the men walked further inland on an almost impassable road over mountains and valleys for 14 miles. It was a fatiguing walk, and they were glad when they reached the banks of the Guaraú River where they rested for a couple of hours and had a bite to eat from their saddle packs.

The prospect for land in this area didn't seem very promising, so they headed upriver in canoes and came to another *fazenda*, where they were told they could acquire food and rest. John and Joseph Matthews were the first to arrive at the home of Senhor Ruibora. The men found that even though they didn't speak the language, they were warmly welcomed into the Ruibora home.

Their interpreter soon arrived and arranged for the group to stay overnight. A sprinkle of rain had now turned into a considerable downpour. The entire group retired about 8 p.m. after eating a comforting meal. As John dozed off, he marveled at the hospitality the entire household had shown to perfect strangers. John reminisced about the platitude of American southerners' hospitality and knew that it'd be hard for any family to top the kindness this family had shown to total strangers who were uneducated in their language and customs. John was grateful for the family and other settlers who had treated them so kindly.

The next morning the team explored the landing area a little more and had planned to set off, but the weather continued to be perilous, so they returned to the Ruibora *fazenda* to spend the better part of the day watching rain fall intermittently throughout the day. They went to bed early, planning to shove off again at midnight and continue their journey to Iguape. They traveled the river for about 18 miles before they stopped at the home of a small coffee planter for a brief respite. Once they got to the River Ribeira, they exchanged their canoes and continued upriver for about 20 more miles. When they stopped for the day at about 7 p.m., they were still several miles from their planned destination. None of the men could say that they were pleased with this part of Brazil.

The rest of the trek to Iguape took the travelers along small river lagoons, lakes, and sea beaches interspersed with mountains. They were in continued agreement that the topography of the area wouldn't be suitable to them nor the other families they represented in the search. The land was generally low and marshy, except where the mountains sloped to the sea. The mountainous land wasn't considered to be suitable for cultivation. Additionally, they found the mosquitos and gnats an extreme nuisance.

Later in the day, the weary cadre arrived in the city and immediately went to their separate hotel rooms for much-needed rest. John endeavored again to catch up on his journal writing as he mused disagreeably about the drizzling rain and reminisced about previous rainy Novembers back home, not his favorite time of year.

The next morning John woke with his journal still in his hand. He joined Dr. Punto and Dan Hall for a walk around Iguape and was introduced to several prominent citizens. Iguape was a small town of about 500 houses and one large church, which was named after a priest who had been buried there. John enjoyed Dr. Punto's story of how the church came to be named after the priest.

"The body of the priest was being transported to Compagny for interment when the parties who carried the coffin with the priest's body in it grew tired and a little confused. They mused that the weight had increased as they passed beyond Igaupe so that they weren't able to carry it further in the direction of Compagny. As they traced their steps back, they found the closer they got to Igaupe, the lighter the body of the priest became. At Igaupe their burden had become light as a feather; consequently, they surmised that the priest wanted to be buried in Igaupe. The church now owned a large parcel of land in the city center. The priest who currently presided over the Catholic parish also managed the property of this church and got paid quite well for it.

John was perplexed by the whole notion of Catholicism but was intrigued by the communication from the Spirit to the coffin bearers in the story and responded with his standard "You don't say?" which was, of course, an idiom that had probably been translated in sundry ways throughout their journey.

At evening tea, the group met an Englishman named Mr. Scorel who had for years resided in Penna. Scorel introduced the woman with him as his wife, but John later learned that she was his traveling companion. They had just returned from a trip to the Guaraú region where he'd looked at some land with the intention of purchasing a new home place.

John sat and listened to stories of old Iguape until his head began to nod—stories of fighting French, Spanish, and Portuguese pirates who all claimed the area as their special place for hoarding. One story related that the city was founded by the Spanish who developed strong relationships with the Tupiniquin Indians and used their knowledge of the area to help look for gold in the rivers. The name Iguape was supposedly taken from the *Tupi* concept of being a river in a cove.

In more recent history, rice had become a mainstay, with rice fields on all sides of the city. The rice of the Iguape region was a quality crop in high demand. It had been the main export crop of the region for 100 years, with much of it being shipped to Europe. In more recent years, Emperor Dom Pedro II, who was still seated as emperor of Brazil, had approved the building of a channel, connecting the river port in the west with the marine port in the east, making transportation easier and more complete.

At noon the following day, some of the men set out in a large canoe for Cananea. Major Hall chose to stay behind at the hotel as he had no interest in this leg of the trip. It became apparent to the rest quickly that the Major's decision may have been a sound one. The men rowed up the *Mar Pequeño*, meaning "little sea," but it was nothing more than an inlet of the ocean.

Toward evening the men tied up their canoes and had a simple pre-arranged supper. While they ate, they listened again to a reverberating thunderstorm. They set out the next morning continuing to Cananea and arrived at about 9 p.m., exhausted and still looking for accommodations for the evening. It was midnight before they were able to settle into sleeping quarters.

The land along the *Mar Pequeño* was barely above tide water; the soil was sandy and poor. There were several small houses and huts along the river. The inhabitants appeared to John to be a racial mixture of Indian and White. They made their living by fishing. Also, there were frequent patches of grape vines, and a few houses had a smattering of coffee trees planted around them. John thought the people didn't look healthy, and when he inquired, he found that many suffered from chills on a regular basis. The land in this area, with only a few exceptions, was carved up into lagoons. It was low and wet.

Just as the men thought they'd seen enough, word came to the group that an American was living nearby who had requested that the travelers visit with him. In a short time, the men found themselves in the home of Captain Alfonse Bulhow, formerly of the Confederate States. Captain Bulhow was presently in the employment of the Brazilian government as a civil engineer, engaged in surveying in that part of the country and was locating a road from Cananea to Curitiba.

Bulhow offered the group breakfast which they heartily accepted, and Mrs. Bulhow began preparing it. Bulhow could access horses for the group to continue the tour, but it would take another day to get them. The men were shown around the small-town area where the most interesting building was a 300-year-old church made of mud and sticks and whitewashed on the outside. They learned that the priest of the church was the biological father to many of the children seen playing in the streets near it. About four months before the group's arrival there had been a scourge, something likened to dysentery that killed almost a quarter of the 400 population of the town and had impacted other towns in the countryside as well.

The group walked about two miles to the Port of the Colony of Cananea. The harbor was good; the bay about 1,000 feet wide and 20 to 30 feet deep. The scouting party was introduced to Mr. Welhro Grocte who owned the only house in the area and who provided lunch and horses. From there the group departed to visit Mr. G.A. Smith, the director of the colony. Mrs. Smith, who was a woman of French heritage, prepared dinner and Mr. Smith welcomed them all to his table.

As they left Cananea, the group saw that the land continued to be low and swampy, but within a short time, it transformed into mountains and valleys. It was drier and appeared to have a high-quality soil. The only problem that John saw was that the land would have to be broken up before it could even be plowed.

The locals called the land *terra roxa;* it was a reddish-purple color something like a vegetable beet. When the soil wasn't this purple color, it was yellow which reminded John of the best cotton land back home. After six miles or so, they came to the house of Mr. Vanderhoof's who was to guide them to the Guaraú River about 12 miles away. On this leg of the journey, John saw land available for sale that he thought would be good for a coffee plantation, as they'd seen a young coffee plantation of about 500 acres, which had trees only three years old that were producing in abundance — so much so that the owner was planning to plant 1,000 more acres immediately.

When they reached the River Guaraú they left the horses behind and once again boarded a canoe to go upriver to observe the sawmill of Bulhow Toltern and Hanson, of great interest to John since his strongest consideration for Brazil was to establish a sawmill. The circular saw blade of the mill was propelled by water. It seemed to work well; however, John was concerned, as he'd been about earlier mill observations, trying to determine how he could maximize the business. The mill was fine as it was for the general vicinity, but to make any real money, he knew they needed a bigger market.

The only way to a bigger market was by the River Guaraú, which was small and mountainous and the Jacupiranga River, which was larger, but which John knew less well at this point. On either of these rivers only a high-water level would be sufficient for a raft or flatboat, and, even then, guidance would be of concern since the river was swift and full of bends and curves. The rise and fall of the rivers also presented a concern. John was glad that they'd arrived in time to see the mill working. As nightfall approached they headed to the home of Mr. and Mrs. Hanson, where they spent the night.

John learned that Mr. Hanson had been clerk of a steamboat on the Alabama River and that his wife was from Selma, although she assured him that she knew the Mobile area well. Mrs. Smith appeared to be quite a young woman and had a daughter who looked to be about three years old. The family had been in Brazil for nine months.

John was intrigued by the various relationship stories he was introduced to in his travels. There were never any explanations regarding any age differences, ethnicity, or racial differences. It was as if any relationship, upon agreement, was acceptable. While John couldn't imagine being in a married relationship outside his race, he was starting to accept that such a liaison might work for some, in which case he was beginning to feel a bit less judgmental. He was developing an appreciation for the fact that social tension in Brazil seemed more likely to be rooted in economics as opposed to ethnicity. When the travelers woke the next morning, Mrs. Smith had prepared coffee, hot rolls, and delicious butter for breakfast.

After their butter-biscuit breakfast, the group canoed down the Jacupiranga to meet Senhor Manes, who was Portuguese by birth but had lived in Brazil for 31 years. John surmised that Manes was a bit over 50 at the time of their meeting and a wealthy gentleman with 80,000 acres of land, 50 slaves, and money in the bank in Portugal. He was a generous host and shared a variety of information with John and Joseph. Manes had a small sugar cane field that was as fine as any John had ever seen. Manes said that he limited the sugar cane to that field because he planted only for what he needed for consumption on his property and not as a consumable.

At noon the next day, Senhor Manes provided canoes and four Negroes to paddle. They passed down the Jacupiranga to the River Turvo, which was a stream about the size of the Bogue Chitto in the general area of John's farm back home. They traveled for about 10 more miles before trading the canoes for horses and mules, then headed out overland again, taking five hours to go 12 miles over deplorable mountain roads complete with washouts. The travel was made even more treacherous when moving slowly down one of the slopes, John's saddle became unfastened, tossing him right over the mule's head. Fortunately, he was able to land on his feet, and apart from a slightly twisted knee, seemed to be unhurt.

The party spent a much-needed evening of rest at the townhome of Senhor Franarnco. The next day they observed the small village of Xirarca, situated on the banks of the Rio Ribeira, then walked just less than a mile along the river to the *fazenda* of Senhor Franarnco where they were greeted by Franarnco, his young wife, and four grown daughters.

After breakfast and a short visit, the group headed back to town and once again loaded into canoes for Caracanga, a plantation owned by Miguel Jorge. When they arrived at 7 p.m., they found the family wasn't home. They bunked overnight, and the next morning headed on to Punto Grasso where Jorge and his family were currently visiting. After several stops, the travelers arrived at 8 p.m. in the cold rain.

Miguel Jorge was a man about 55 years old, while his wife appeared to be nearer 25. John noticed right away that Jorge's wife was his darling, but John thought the way she dressed, and her mannerism marked her as overly flirtatious. She was talkative and carried on as much conversation as the language barrier would permit. The couple was very hospitable, and their young child played contentedly around the visitors' feet. Joe Matthews thought Jorge to be a bit pompous, but John just saw him as confident and open with his opinions.

Senhor Jorge provided the crew with a new canoe, a huge and fine one, as the one they'd picked up in Xirarca was inferior. As they shoved off for the mouth of the Iporanga and returned to Iguape, they were accompanied by Senhor Moraus, who was the uncle of Jorge's wife. While they passed down the Ribeira River, they stopped from time to time to look at the land and concluded that much of the land along the river was alluvial, but they also saw the *terra roxa* and yellow clay. Some of the river banks extended 20 feet high, but most were less than 10. Moraus explained that the river flooded every five to seven years, but that the water would recede in four to five days, which made rice the perfect crop for the Ribeira region.

They reached the mouth of the Iporanga about 7:30 p.m. and were given refuge from the rain by a merchant friend of Moraus. Here they learned that they would need to wait out the weather as the wind was driving the water upstream. Finally, at noon the next day, the wind subsided enough that the men could resume their tour. John had grown weary of the blowing rain, but he thought he'd never forget the kindness of Moraus and the vision of him standing on the river bank waving goodbye until they were entirely out of sight.

They arrived at Iguape after dark, and again the rain was falling. The land along the river in this section had been very similar to what they'd seen the day before. As the river banks became lower, they could see Brazilian homes here and there along the way. Many of the smaller houses were raised or built on posts so that they were out of the water.

The men saw that the land nearest the banks was the highest as it sloped from the river and created lagoons or swamps. Much to his surprise, John learned that steamboats could navigate the Ribeira to Xirarca where it was 200 feet wide; however, the fall in the river rendered it unnavigable at that point.

They stayed at Iguape for two days before heading out on the last leg of the sojourn back to Santos, which would take them the better part of six days — canoeing the Ribeira at first, walking two miles along the sea beach, then on down the river for 30 miles by canoe, four miles over the Mina Mountain, followed by eight more miles on the Gueraher River, six more miles over the Guaramba mountain to Pinuabe.

Pinuabe was a small village of about 50 houses where the travelers acquired mules and carts, then traveled 24 miles to Cananéia, finally by mules and oxen for 12 miles to another river, which led them to the 24 miles of beach to Santos where they arrived at 6:30 p.m. on August 31, 1866.

John rested two days in Santos before taking the train back to São Paulo. Upon arriving in São Paulo, he checked into the Hotel Europa, where he planned to remain for a week or so, taking the time to check the pulse of everyone he could in that community to be sure that he was factoring in all the details from his fellow travelers and from Americans who had already moved to Brazil.

He had met several men who were already settling in — Col. Bowen and Mr. Russell of Texas, Mr. Burney of South Carolina, and the Reverend Dunn of New Orleans, who expected to attract a large contingent to his colony. Dunn, who had been the rector of St. Phillips Church in New Orleans before the war, was concluding his second visit to Brazil. He'd come the preceding October as well. He seemed very pleased with the land he had identified on one of the tributaries of the Ribeira. Dunn was heading out on the next steamboat bound for the U.S. to organize the relocation of several families.

John learned that Major McMullen was back in the United States after visiting the family and friends of Col. Bowen, who seemed pleased with the new prospects, although they reported that the Major said he wouldn't be planting cotton because he didn't believe it would do well. John agreed; he felt there was too much rain below the *serra* to grow cotton or coffee. Again, rice, he thought, would do well.

The Interlude

The bond between Kate Teal and John Foster formed quickly, and, some would speculate dangerously. There were philosophical, ethical, and emotional reasons for Kate to keep her distance from John Foster, but the attraction between the two was all powerful. Time itself took on an ethereal quality when they were together — it seemed like a lifetime; it seemed like a fleeting moment.

While John explored financial and property matters of moving his family and neighbors to Brazil, Kate enjoyed getting the school ready for teaching, but she also knew the school wouldn't fully support her and that money could become an issue quickly. Because the school was fledgling, and her salary was only a stipend, except for the fact that she was allowed residence in the cottage, Kate found it necessary to bring in additional income in other small ways.

She found a merchant in the center of town who would sell, on consignment, the flowers she bundled from her garden, which was coming along well. She learned the local flora strictly by experiment. Her best resource, past the yardman for the church, was a marketplace located on fertile land just a short distance from town where she could purchase local seeds that fed her experimentation. She supplied another merchant with small patchwork designs that she'd begun working to calm the incessant thinking that she fell into from time to time. She was amused that her therapy would help to sustain her in more ways than one.

Kate crammed the remaining few items in the basket, wondering why she was always in a bit of a rush, and threw the brightly colored tablecloth over the top of the cold dinner that she'd pulled together of leftover fried chicken, cold biscuits, honey, fig tarts, grapes, and a cask of South American wine.

It was mid-afternoon when John tied the horses that pulled the small carriage he'd borrowed to a small tree in her front yard. She anticipated the sound of his voice whether it was a matter of fact, teasing, or admiring. It was like pine and jasmine on a chilly morning. There was something intimately familiar and comforting in it. He was whistling a tune as she stepped onto her porch.

"Did you have any trouble finding the place?"

"Not at all after I figured out the last left turn you told me to take was a right turn," he teased.

"Oh no!"

"Oh yes! But here is a thing you need to know," he said with the full authority of his presence. "I'll always be able to find you. Always."

"You sound mighty sure of yourself."

"I'm sure of a lot of things, Kate, and this is one of them."

They both laughed. They felt comfortable with each other. Sharing this level of comfort with another was like nothing either had ever experienced before.

They exited the wagon path. John directed the horses pulling the carriage to a far back corner of a sugarcane field where a large Brazilian Rosewood with bowing branches leaned down to touch the earth. John gave a cursory look for varmints, pulled a blanket from the back of the carriage, and spread it perfectly square. He returned to the carriage, picked up the basket of food, and reached for Kate's hand to steady her footing as she eased her way out of the carriage.

There on the blanket at the edge of the cane field, they talked for hours. John seemed to need to tell Kate about himself—the bad along with the good.

Kate knew that one of the things people need most in the world is to have someone who knows them fully, and she could see that this knowledge was at least one of the things John wanted from her.

She stood in front of him leaning back against his chest as they watched the sun slip below the rim of the earth. When the peach horizon was all but gone, he kissed her behind each ear and then the top of her shoulders. He tugged at her blouse. She loosened it and met him with the intensity he brought to her. It had been years since Kate had been physically intimate with a man, and she was somewhat surprised to find how quickly all her senses were reawakened. She was fully alive, accepting every touch, resisting nothing. His warm whisper against her ear alone was enough to ignite her world.

When she caught her breath, she lay still for some time, then gently opened her eyes to see dancing fireflies. "Look John, lightning bugs, dozens of them."

"Yes, I think they're putting on a show for you!"

Propped up on her elbows she leaned over to kiss him lightly on the cheek. "Well, I think you were putting on a show for them!" They both laughed.

"Lie back." He gently lowered her head to the blanket. "I want to count the stars in your eyes." She blushed and smiled.

"John, I'm not sure, but earlier, during all the activity, I thought I heard a bear. It said, "woof woof.""

"Woof, woof, isn't that a dog?"

"Yes, but a bear sounds like it's imitating a dog, and I think I heard one!"

"I think you did too."

"Are you kidding? We could've been eaten alive! I thought it was just my imagination."

"I think the bear knew to stay away… too much activity. I don't think the bear wanted any part of what was going on here a few minutes ago." They both laughed aloud.

He pulled Kate to her feet, helped her to adjust her clothing, and with a hand on each side of her head, he fluffed her hair a bit. They shared a lingering kiss, then John gave her an easy twirl, put his hand on her waist and gently began to waltz to the music of the newly appearing stars. She leaned into him as he sighed in her ear, "Kate you're so very special to me."

When she woke the next morning, it seemed as if the previous evening had been a dream. As she lay in her bed fading in and out of sleep, she indulged herself by replaying the images from the night before. She didn't regret anything and wouldn't allow herself to think any further than the present moment.

When she got up, she threw on her walking shoes, pulled her hair back, and without even a cup of coffee headed out for a walk. She walked at a steady pace until she reached the edge of the first cane field that bordered the town. The morning sun was burning through the low, heavy clouds causing the dew drops from the early morning to glisten like cut diamonds as they clung to the slender leaves on the stalks. The humidity was already intense. She leaned her face into the stalks and breathed deeply, "Poetry insists on existing."

Kate had never been happier than the days she spent with John. The air between them was charged with uplifting energy. She realized the two together were quite the paradox. Theirs wasn't a relationship that would make much sense to anyone who knew either of them well. They had so much in common that one seemed to echo the other, but had so little in common when it came to the big issues of organized religion and politics. He was highly conservative and traditional in this thinking on those topics. She was much more opened-ended in her thinking and personal philosophies.

One would wonder how they could tolerate each other at all, but there was mutual respect for the other's outlook that carried them through to the other side. Kate was amazed at how they could spend hours talking about life and never get into a riff over the other's belief system. John's boldness sometimes bordered on what Kate thought was extreme. She had a great distaste for arrogance but somehow could accept that facet of character as part of who he was. It had been clear to her for a long time now that you never get the whole story from the facts. For both, practicality had taken precedence over everything else for so long that the freedom to dream was a beautiful indulgence. Simple conversations went on for hours and engulfed the two, causing them to lose all track of schedules.

Kate had never known a man who seemed so genuinely interested in what she thought, even though on those important topics of difference, her thoughts appeared to impact him minimally if at all. She asked him, "Why do you say, 'talk to me'; 'tell me something?'

To which he replied, "I want to share everything with you, and I believe you enjoy the sharing as well. I relish the reciprocation that happens between us and have great anticipation about what your responses to my questions will be."

Kate knew that she sometimes saw things a little differently, but never thought of her comments in this way. However, she did always enjoy the unexpected as it unfolded when she was rambling on about one thing or another. The two of them together was an entirely unexpected occurrence. In the interlude, perhaps it was the peace they found in each other that made them compatible beyond anything either of them had known.

Kate registered an awareness of her breath; it was deep and steady. She noticed how her belly filled as she inhaled. She thought, how wonderful it was to feel at peace as she contemplated her feelings for John. Love is the whetstone that sharpens the senses, allows one to see color more brilliantly, causes food to taste sweeter, spicier. Love makes life more evident, right down to the breath that hangs on the air of a cool morning.

After spending most of the day exploring the city, its parks, little cafes and alleyways, the late afternoons and evenings were spent lounging through the evening meal recapping the day, or telling each other stories that for the most part, astonishingly, focused on the simplest things in life.

Even though John had confirmed from the locals that August had been one of the rainiest months in memory, and he'd grown weary of it on the scouting trek, he appreciated the light rain they were experiencing now.

Considering there was less rainfall in September than one might find in Alabama, Kate and John were enchanted by a drizzle as they enjoyed a late breakfast of ham and biscuits in a small restaurant situated at an angle in a small alley not too far from Kate's new home. They found a table near an open window, so they could watch the morning rain while they drank their café and waited for the *presunto* and *biscoito*. This was the first time that either of them had traveled to a country where they didn't speak the primary language.

As they placed their order with the young man waiting on the table, Kate endeavored to communicate by writing. Since she'd forgotten her translation book, she struggled with the word for ham. John went right into charades imitating a pig. The waiter was a bit confused, but when John laughed at himself, they all burst out laughing. The waiter walked away saying *'Presunto! Presunto!'* As they settled in, waiting for their food, the two were quiet, a quiet that was comfortable and relaxing, as opposed to a strained or an indifferent quiet that sometimes exists between two people. There was a language all its own in their silence.

She asked one question, "Don't you love the smell of the rain?"

"Yes, especially when you catch the scent of it before it falls."

"As if the scent were a presentiment."

"How's your friend Notch getting along?"

"Ah, Notch is off on a grand new adventure. He wasn't sure of his destination, I mean, whether he'd return to Brazil or go back to Mississippi, but for now, he's going to explore the origin of his French ancestors. I know he plans to visit Chateau de Malmaison. The property appears to be back in the Bonaparte family currently. I don't know if Notch is expecting a tour, but he'll probably find a way to get one!" she laughed.

"France! I thought his Grandfather Leflore was from Canada."

"He was, but the French Canadians, of course, originated in France. Notch is interested in the possibility of tobacco exports from America to France. He was inspired by the exports here in Brazil; this country exports tobacco to France as well. He believes if he can see first-hand what happens in production, as he has done here, and resell on the receiving end, he can determine a profitable way to engage in the process. Both he and I have been reading or rather have some of the locals read to us from the French newspapers. It amazes me how many people here seem to know multiple languages, at least enough of each one to communicate the basics."

"Before he left, he went to back to Rio for six weeks and worked in a French bakery. How Notch found out about the employment, I never understood, but knowing him, he may have just shown up at their door as if that was where he was supposed to be, and it felt the same to the baker. I'm sure there must be some English spoken in Paris, but he wanted to be a little better prepared when he arrived than we were when we arrived in Brazil. Notch shared with me that most of the workers in the bakery were family members of the owner Blanchard, so they were native French speakers. Notch adopts language quickly, a real gift if you ask me. He has always been concerned about the inevitable loss of his native language. He says we lose the diversity of thinking when we lose our language—ways of description, problem-solving, and appreciation."

"He did come for a visit about a week before he set out on his newest voyage. He helped me get settled in the cottage and made sure I had everything I needed for these mild winter months that we know as summer. I find the reversal of seasons one of the hardest adjustments. Well, anyway, we had a wonderful picnic by the lake a couple of days before he left. It was a bit cool, but a beautiful sunny day."

John interrupted, "You and Notch are quite the pair, aren't you? Makes me a little suspicious of the relationship, but I guess that's none of my business."

"No, it isn't any of your concern, but as I've said before, Notch and I've been in lockstep all of our lives. I'm not sure what makes it so, but I'm the kind of gal who can have relationships with men outside the romantic and physical, even though there can be an exception." She flashed a mischievous smile. "Notch is a brother in the deepest emotional sense."

"I'm sure he is," John mumbled and then changed the subject. "I did see tobacco growing on a couple or the *fazendas* on the scouting journey. I'm telling you, Kate, one of the greatest problems this country has is transportation. It's a huge challenge getting their crops of all kinds from the plantations to the market."

Kate went on. "I haven't had a letter from Notch yet, and I do look forward to hearing what he thinks after he sees the demolition and reconstruction going on in Paris as part of what they're calling the Second French Empire. I cannot even imagine going to such a big city. It's filled with poverty and the way they bury poor people is an abomination. I don't know; this may sound crazy, but I think city poverty would be something I couldn't abide. Mind you, I've experienced poverty, but even when you're penniless in the countryside, there's some dignity, where I see none when people are crowded into small spaces, dwellings one on top of the other by the hundreds."

"That does sound very bleak."

"Wide open spaces may indeed be a luxury. Sorry for revealing so much fear, I'm sure there are wonderful things in the city, of course! I've asked Notch to send word about the art that pours out of Paris. There's Claude Monet, a newcomer I find very interesting for the way he captures nature. The people in his paintings seem secondary to the natural world he engages. I appreciate Édouard Manet's *Music in Tuileries*. He also has some controversial pieces, but when it comes to instigating judgments, there's Gustave Courbet, who's causing a great stir with his painting of two women along the Seine, not to mention one he calls something like 'The Origin of the World.'" Kate burst out laughing.

"What's the laughing all about? How could a painting about the origin of the world be so funny?"

"Well John, the origin of the world is a bit erotic, and I'm sure I shouldn't go there with you, not over breakfast anyway, but somehow can't help myself." She continued laughing.

"Well, explain."

"I'm sure I can't explain. You'll have to do your perusal of Parisian art. Maybe after dark." She laughed again.

John was amused by her comments and the blush that rushed across her cheeks. He wouldn't press her now, but he'd make a mental note to come back to this topic 'after dark.' "I've meant to ask you about this. Notch was always saying some greeting or phase to me, Choctaw, I suppose, when we met on the deck of the *Isabella*."

Kate was full of herself this morning. She laughed again and said a little sarcastically, "Well, of course, it was a greeting, it wasn't a curse. He thought it'd be good for you to hear something a little different. For Notch, it was a playful annoyance. Notch likes to tease. The term was *Chim achukma* and it means 'How are you?' as in a friendly greeting."

"What do you mean, though it would be good for me to hear something different? I'm an open-minded fellow."

"John, my dear." She folded his perception up softly in her voice, "You may not be as open-minded as you think you are. The world is very diverse. Please don't take these comments as insults, but for both of us, John, there's so much to learn. It's a compliment that Notch teased you. He likes you. He doesn't take the time, to engage everyone. I'm going to miss him terribly."

John shifted the subject to tell Kate more about his scouting journey. "We saw a vast array of landscapes, from large craggy mountains to seashore. Fertile land and poor soil. I thought

Alabama had a lot of rivers! We crossed a river on every leg of the journey, some days we took canoes up rivers. The transportation in this country is going to have to improve if they want Americans to move down here. That first train ride you experienced over from Rio was nothing compared to what's beyond the city out there. And ants, I've never seen so many ants! You know, I fell off my mule one day? Sure did! Went right over his head. Lucky for me I landed, well, basically landed, on my feet. I do think some locations will make for good homesteads. I'm checking into title issues and sale prices on a couple of them."

"Early one evening, when I was waiting for some of the others to catch up, I sat on a river bank and just watched the water flow. Crazy, I know, but I do that sometimes. You love me, anyway don't you?" He squeezed Kate's arm playfully. "So, as I sat there watching the river flow, I noticed a single leaf that was floating down the stream, merrily, merrily, merrily. I thought how happy it seemed moving along at its own pace, not bound up in clusters against the bank like other leaves. This leaf seemed to have its own rhythm, moving on its own. At that moment, I found that little leaf to be, as you say, inspiring."

"Ah, I haven't been much of a woodswoman." Kate laughed at her label. "But I've been an observer and lover of the natural world for as long as I can remember. Before Notch left, we took a picnic to the Lake Ibirapuera. While he swam, I propped myself against the trunk of a huge Brazilian Rosewood and read some of R.W. Emerson's essays. The sweet scent of the tree, reminiscent of roses themselves, seemed such an indulgence. There are so many beautiful flowering trees in this country. Being able to immerse myself in them is such a gift. Near where I sat, a grand pink Paineira, whose canopy reflected in the lake like a cradle rising out of it, was the most beautiful tree I've ever seen. It was laden with lily-like blooms. And, John, now I understand why some of the flowers have such a dear price at the market — the tree trunks are covered with dense thorns, not unlike roses back home, but much larger. Gathering these blooms would take skill and bodily protection."

"After Notch and I snacked on the sweet muffins and goat cheese, we sat together in thanks and prayed for safety and guidance as we each went forward in these new ways. As we sat together in prayer, everything around us was perfectly still—the reeds, the grasshoppers, the birds were still and silent. At the exact moment that each of us drew in a deep replenishing breath and gradually let it go, the air began to stir, and the trees filled with a rising symphony of birdsong. To me, John, this experience was an affirmation that we're not separate from nature, but rather a part of it. I drifted off for a short nap, and when I woke, I found that Notch had placed flower blossoms and buds all around me. How sweet is that?"

"Sweet, yeah," he added, with a hint of sarcasm. "What kind of prayer did Notch pray?"

"Whatever he chose."

"What do you mean? He's Christian, right."

"Yes, he's Christian, but his Christianity does not limit his experience as a spiritual member of an ancient Choctaw people."

"I'm not sure if I know what you mean and to be quite candid, Kate, sometimes I worry about your soul."

"John, my soul is taken care of. You needn't worry about that."

"You've been baptized in the Holy Spirit?"

"Yes, I've been baptized. It was the way of my family. But if there's one thing I know for sure by the way that life has presented itself to me is that God is bigger than I thought, bigger than most people think. I believe that the presence of God presents itself to groups of people in various time periods and geographies in a way that they can best comprehend the presence. I mean, really John, why should I trust my immortal soul to anyone else's interpretation of God?"

"Well, I believe that there's only one way to heaven."

"I know you do, John, and I'm not going to try to convince you otherwise. Consequently, I'm not spending my breath on this conversation. I know there's an unexpected difference between intelligence and enlightenment."

John recognized that her comment was criticism, and he stammered to overlook it, but another thought preoccupied him. "I'm sure I shouldn't mention such specifics to you, but among the correspondence, I've received when I returned from this last scouting expedition, was a letter from Cynthia. The letter was filled with heaviness—all about who has passed on—died, you know, more neighbors losing their farms and such. I know these are real concerns, and I don't disregard the fact that there're many issues that I must deal with, but there wasn't one word in the note about her missing me, not one question as to my well-being, not one comment that suggested that I'm any more than the designated problem solver. I'm the provider and the problem solver, and I take such responsibility seriously. I wish she were ... never mind. I've said too much already."

Kate replied merely, "I never allow myself to forget that Cynthia exists, even on our best days. Back to your scouting journey, John, what do your colleagues think of slavery in this country?"

"There's an abundance of slaves in the countryside—huge numbers of Negro slaves from Africa. There are slaves from the local Indian population, and even at one Fazenda, a contingency of Germans who weren't treated much differently from the slave population. For the most part, the relationships between the planters and the slaves seemed entrenched in a compliant way."

"But, still they are slaves."

"But still they are slaves. I observed Vergueiro, a coffee planter, using a more benevolent method of managing his slaves by providing more than adequate clothing for men, women, and children alike and providing an office, regularly visited by a physician, for the dispensation of medicine. Another planter expressed that the best way to get the most from the slaves was to employ little or no corporal punishment and provide them with plenty to eat; however, I must add that I saw some disturbing situations as well. At one locale, we could hear movement in shackles before we saw them—a group of slaves was being made to work in shackles as punishment for some disobedience. The image that I couldn't get out of my mind was that of an ancient woman in ankle shackles while she was stirring the coffee beans that were drying. I wondered what in the world the old woman could have done to deserve such treatment."

"The gentlemen who are coming to Brazil to re-establish themselves as planters are pleased with the slavery situation in Brazil, but some contemplate, in more private settings, that they may be jumping from the frying pan into the fire. There's some talk about the inevitability of dissolution of the institution of slavery. While no one seems to expect that such a change would produce the bloodbath that the United States experienced, I have to say that there are an estimated 2,000,000 Negro slaves in Brazil. They aren't only located on isolated plantations. They are everywhere. The women are in towns of any size at all, selling fruits and vegetables, fish, pottery and the like. Almost every operation of any size—brick making to kitchen help has slaves attached to the production. The argument is that the slaves and slavers are at peace now and no entities are pressing too hard for any change, but what happens if that changes and Brazil erupts? Some say that if the Empire of Brazil, at some point in the future, decides to emancipate the slaves, that the powerful Brazilian aristocracy would do everything possible to guarantee the transition from slave labor to free labor smoothly. This concerns me, Kate. Who can guarantee such a thing?"

Pocket Knife

On some days, Kate and John ventured over to a city park. As they sat on the shaded wooden bench in the park trying to identify various bird calls, he peeled an orange for her with his pocket knife. Kate reflected briefly on the dinner in St. Thomas with Notch's comments about her needing some spoiling. Having someone peel your fruit for you seemed to be the highest form of indulgence, Kate thought.

"So, what about this pocket knife John? I know men are very partial to their pocket knives." "You're so right, Mrs. Teal. They are. A pocket knife is one of a man's most prized possessions. My father gave this knife to me. It belonged to his brother who passed when he was a young man. A horse they were trying to break kicked him in the head. The blow killed him instantly. But this knife here has been good luck for me, helping me through some task almost every day, sometimes through small tasks, sometimes through something much larger. So, My Dear, this knife I'm putting into your tiny hand is a Sheffield Folding Bowie. It was made almost 30 years ago. It's a folding Bowie. Now, don't get too excited when I say, Bowie. This knife didn't belong to the famous Jim Bowie who died at the Alamo in '36 but is designed in a similar fashion to his knife. It has not one but two folding blades, and as you can see, they're getting pretty thin from wear over the years." John looked up directly into her blue eyes, "I'm like this knife; I'm getting' old." He broke the silence with a laugh, "But, I'm still here now!" Kate laughed with him. "You see, Kate, the blades wear away with all the sharpening over the years. The handle is made of deer horn. Weathered like it is, it could be mistaken for pecan tree bark, couldn't it? Iron pins and an iron bolster binds the pieces together."

"I remember hearing my Grandpa Powell talking about using pieces of broken larger blades from handsaws, cross cut saws, and the like to make his pocket knives. I hear it gave him confidence well beyond his stature. Some bigger fragments of the larger blades were used to make kitchen knives, adding oak and hickory handles. Nothing went to waste; it was a good lesson to learn. A man's conviction of confidence serves to make him a powerful force. I was too young to know the story firsthand, but I can remember hearing about my Grandfather approaching his son-in-law, my Uncle George after he struck my Aunt Elizabeth across the face. Grandpa Powell called Uncle George to the front door of their small house and showed him the knife he carried in his back right pocket. He explained in no uncertain terms that if he ever hit my aunt again, he'd never so much as look at another woman, and if he did, there'd be nothing he could do about it. Grandpa Powell died when I was quite young. I wish I had had the chance to know him better."

Kate changed the subject abruptly. "While you were away, I learned that São Paulo's origin is very old, even though it has only a few significant structures, which are the churches of course—the church and convent of Luz, the Carmo Church, and Sao Francisco Church. We have no structures this old at home. Jesuit missionaries founded it in the mid-1500s on the date the Catholic Church holds as the anniversary of the conversion of St. Paul; therefore, the city's name. The exact location of the founding of the city has a school and church called *Pateo do Collegio*, which is Portuguese for the schoolyard. I visited there before I met the Powers. I found it not to be a good fit for me, but somehow love knowing that it exists."

"The best that I could understand, the workers around the schoolyard said the building was made of rammed earth. I've never heard the term, but the construction looked like what I'd expect some of the structures in the western territories of the United States to look like," Kate said.

"Rammed earth, yes, I'm sure I know basically what that means. It's the use of natural raw materials. Could be clay earth, chalk, lime, gravel, any dense, naturally available composite. It's an ancient way of building and requires significant labor to pound the materials into a solid foundation, walls, and floors. Possible water damage is the biggest concern of this type of construction. Building with wood is much easier, particularly if you have a sawmill," John said.

Kate looked at John quizzically for a full second, then burst out laughing. She went on with her story. She'd learned that the big house at the center of the city with its colonial attributes was called the *Solar of the Marquise of Santos*. The marquise, who is Domitila de Castro Canto e Melo, is an elderly woman, who still lives in the home. I was surprised to learn that in the early part of the century, she was the lover of Dom Pedro I, who conferred the title of marchioness upon her.

"I for one, given my relationship with you John, shouldn't get so involved in telling tales. Forgive me if you think what I have to say is gossip. I'm not interested in placing value on Domitila's actions or Dom Pedro's for that matter. It's just all fascinating to me —how relationships work in this country, I mean. Dom Pedro had several other romantic relationships, some simultaneously, but this woman, Domitila, is said to have been the most important one. The emperor never married her. He did marry twice. His second wife, Amélie of Leuchtenberg was the granddaughter of Napoleon Bonaparte's wife, Empress Josephine. Aren't the politics of the relationships interesting? Dom Pedro bestowed several official titles upon Domitila including marchioness, and the two had children together, as well as children by other relationships."

"Emperor Dom Pedro behaves like this?"

"Not Dom Pedro, the current emperor, but his father."

"His father? Well, that's not right."

"So, John Foster, how many wives do you think a man should have?"

He gasped and turned to her as if to speak swiftly, but when he saw the expression on her face, raised his eyebrows. He quickly understood that she was speaking of their relationship and his marriage. He was quiet and finally said quietly, "OK."

"This area of town is called the *Triangula*, the Triangle, which is the city's center, so I can walk there fairly easily for entertainment and shopping for any items I might find necessary."

"Sounds like you're adjusting well."

"Yes, I think I'm becoming a regular *Paulista*."

"A what?"

They both laughed. "A *Paulista*, that's what the locals are called. Some say *Paulistanos*. I don't know John, this is an intriguing place, and it appears to me to be poised for growth. There's a fledgling newspaper that is starting up, *O Estado de São Paulo, The State of* São

Paulo. I'm thinking about approaching the publisher with the notion of writing a column specifically aimed at the *Confederados* and other immigrants, written and published in English, of course. Maybe I'll call the column 'What the Woman Said.' Let me see if I can say this, '*O Que a Mulher Disse,*' or maybe 'She Said What?' — '*Ela Disse o Que?*'" She laughed, "Ok, I'm just showing off now. However, I'm thinking of something along the lines of the Hans Christian Andersen travelogues."

Sawmills

Kate made a tasty supper for them of beef tips drizzled in fig sauce, rice, heart of palm, and chocolate tarts. The meal had taken her all day, but she was excited to have pulled together such a local delicacy and hoped that John would enjoy it. She was excited to share with John how figs were ripe almost all year long in Brazil, how the scent of them made her nostalgic, reminding her of childhood summers in Mississippi, and how she thought she might plant a fig tree at the cottage.

He did enjoy the meal even though the heart of palm was a bit unusual for him. Mostly he loved that Kate had made such a special meal for them. They took their *chimarrão*, which was a version of sweetened tea with orange peel, to the garden. She insisted they drink from a single gourd like a cup with a single straw or *bomba* as the locals called it. This *bomba* was simple, made of bamboo, and Kate explained to John that this version of tea was a product of the Tupi Indians, who now lived at the edge of São Paulo. Sitting side by side, he fingered the bracelet that he noticed she wore almost daily. "This is special to you?" he asked.

"Yes, and of course, there's a story. There's a story for everything. My dear papa gave this to me when I first learned I had been accepted to the Institute for studies. He had his sister in Scotland send it to him, a process which took months, I'm sure. I think he'd been holding on it for some grand occasion, whatever came, first school or marriage." She laughed. "My aunt may have even been the instigator of the whole exchange. When I think of all the effort between the two of them, I love it even more. The bracelet was crafted in Scotland and made popular by Queen Victoria, who loved her visits there. This quartz in the silver setting shaped like a flower is called *Cairngorm* because it's found in the Cairngorm Mountain Range. Look, even though the stone is a yellow-brown, it sparkles like a diamond. When Papa gave me the bracelet he said, 'Now, my Lillian Kate Teal, I know you're all grown up and have a very good head on your shoulders, but I'm giving you this bracelet to be of comfort to you as you venture out into this big old world — the Cairngorm, with all its sparkle is to remind you that even in the darkest days, life is full of beauty and hope; the agates are a reminder that you're a special woman, a strong woman. These simple principles are ones that people often forget, but these, along with your faith, will sustain you wherever you are.'"

"I treasure the bracelet. It'll always be my most valued possession. At first, I was afraid to wear it for fear of damaging or even losing it, but Papa didn't give it to me to rest in a bureau drawer. The qualities with which he imbued the bracelet have indeed comforted me through some difficult periods. As I've contemplated the bracelet in recent times, it has also given me an appreciation that home isn't always just one place. There have been many homes for me, for my family. Although I've never been to Scotland, I'm connected to my grandfather's home through my blood. My family's home near Jackson, where I grew up, gives me solid roots in Mississippi. The bracelet was given to me as I made a temporary home in Tennessee while I studied, then moved to the Thompson farm. Now, here I am in South America rattling on about my jewelry! Enough of you getting me to talk about myself, tell me about the sawmill business, John."

"Before I tell you about the sawmill, I have to tell you a little ghost story," John said.

"I'm not much on being intentionally scared but hold me tight and tell me your story."

"That's the spirit, Kate! This was back in the old days, you know, my younger years." He smiled. "It was a full day's wagon ride from the place I grew up to get supplies we needed for the homestead, and I do mean a full day. My Papa would leave before sunup carrying a cold biscuit and some nuts, maybe some seasonal fruit. He would drive a buckboard all day into town and back. Why, it would be after midnight most times when he returned. When I got to be about 12 or 13, he'd send me on the trek, which had to be made every four or five months or so. You know the old people talk about haints and spirits and such."

"Before I set out on my first trip by my lonesome, Papa told me there was a place about midway on the route where the atmosphere would change, become cooler. Just remove the thought from your pretty little head that there must be a bog or something in the area because there was none. Anyway, the cool air was peculiar in the way it made the hair stand up on the back of your neck and down your arms, you know—goosebumps. The Acadian people over in Louisiana call it the *frissons*. I met one of them fellows once."

"Anyway, Papa said he knew there was a spirit of something dwelling in that area, but he didn't know what kind. When I got to that point where I got the *frissons,* I was to keep steady on the path that I was on, not turn back and not start trying to trace or track anything. Just keep going. He never told me exactly where this spot was, but I tell you more than once, I felt I was not alone for the journey. So, I can tell you I'm a lucky man about the sawmill business and otherwise. I ponder that fact every day and thank God that my small mill was spared destruction."

"Let me back up. I picked up the sawmill notion from my Papa who had tinkered with the idea and had a very small rudimentary setup. As I looked around and saw the area growing, I thought 'now, something the folks can use is more lumber, faster and cheaper', so I set about learning more about the industry. Being so near the Dog River was a real asset to the process. Yellow pine could be floated down the Dog from the thick forests just to the north on down to near my place. Using some cheap labor, including my cousins, a couple of them who became investors of a sort in the mill—that's how I paid them for their efforts."

"Anyway, me and the boys dug a ditch about a mile and a half long and just floated those logs right up to the mill site. We diverted water from the river itself to move the logs. The big ditch, canal, channel, whatever you want to call it, was about four feet wide and three to four feet deep. We stationed poles along the way to help guide the logs along the path. I had a half-dozen mules to pull the heavy timber to the blades. They also pulled the pallets where the boards—the finished products—were stacked and loaded onto skiffs and floated down the river to Mobile."

"What changed the mill was when we added a steam engine about 10 years ago. Now, that's the wave of the future—steam. Did you know that in just 10 years the number of manufacturing businesses, including sawmills using steam, went up by 10%? I bet you didn't know that, did you?" He laughed.

"Well, here's what happened, when factories in the South started building steam engines, they became much more affordable, and sawmill outfits were one of the first business-types to buy into the steam engine concept. I knew I couldn't miss that boat, so I started investigating. I wrote a letter or two to James Young's Iron Works located in Eufaula, in east Alabama. I'd read that the owners were informing themselves on the steam process and were more than willing to work with buyers to design just the thing they needed. I had some kin over in that area and was planning to use them as an excuse to ramble on over there, but then I discovered a foundry near Mobile that was making the steam engines, so that location really made the most sense, although I don't always do what makes the most sense to some folks, I think you know that, or are learning that already." He chuckled.

"These engines don't come cheap, so I purchased an engine on the smaller side, for starters. I had the unit built and hauled over to my place. All this design work and building took several months, but when we had the engine in place, she was a beauty and, even though still somewhat temperamental, made much faster work of the sawing—fast compared to what it had been. Some critics of the steam engines called them sawdust making machines, and I must admit, they do produce some sawdust! You see the way the circular saw sets against the wood takes about a quarter inch of each board, consequently, that's where you get your sawdust. Maybe one day someone will figure out something to do with all that dust. Our output jumped way up, and sales were taking off."

"There's some big engines back home. There was a textile factory on the river in Mobile that had a 200-horsepower steam engine. Now, that's some power. They had a big operation going on with Irish immigrants doing a lot of the work, but the factory burned, accidentally, they say. The parts were scavenged and sold at a low cost to the Confederate Army to reuse in any way they could."

"Why did you say you were lucky?"

"I was lucky because my little mill was spared. What's the $50 word they use?

"In my opinion, Colonel Beard went a little crazy. Not only did we have that Yankee heathen, William Tecumseh Sherman, demolishing infrastructure from Vicksburg to the Alabama line at Meridian, including pulling up railroad ties and the Northern Army occupying the area, but, then we had Colonel Beard, our own colonel, who had launched his personal version of the "scorch and burn" plan ordering all machinery, public and private, which could be used by the enemy, to be destroyed, and that order included sawmills. His two-day raid focused on the Blackwater and Escambia river systems."

"My mill and home are just a short way west of that area. I had an idea that made everybody think I was a little crazy, even me, but I figured I had to do something to protect my investment, our very livelihood. Being a somewhat small outfit made it possible for me to dismantle the operation. I hid parts everywhere, scattered them on both sides of the river banks, thinking if the parts were separated, it would be harder for anyone to deduce that they belonged together. I even sank some big logs we had on the place in the river, mostly big beautiful cypress logs. Being far off the main roads, not on the beaten path to Mobile, and having ceased production weeks earlier gave us good cover. What a time, Kate. We got both sides destroying an industry that makes an economy work."

"I worked the sawmill as long as I could. Every morning I'd fill an old ceramic cup with dark, rich chicory coffee; I mean it would be steaming hot, right off the fire. I'd carry it with me as I walked across the place down to the mill, sipping a little all along as it cooled. Some days, along the walk, I'd reminisce about how my father would sit at the table in the burgeoning light of the morning and pour his coffee, a little at a time, in a saucer to cool it. He'd drink it from the saucer, making a swizzling sound as he went."

"My favorite part of the day, after my morning coffee of course, and listening to the coo of the mourning doves and the call and response of the field larks (a pretty, little brown bird with yellow markings under and above its beak and a black mask over its eyes), was when the saws began running. What I loved about it, Kate, was the smell of wood as it was planed. The soft yellow pine and the cypress were my favorite. And, everybody loves the smell of cedar, you know the wood in lots of storage trunks and chests. It's such a distinct smell, like sweet rosin and rosemary. Then, there was almost, I guess you'd say, a sentimental moment when I latched the big door that enclosed the old barn. A feeling would come over me like I was pulling the door closed on another day of my family's history."

Kate listened to him talk and was silent a few moments. Finally, she said, "It's a nightmare to live in a place that is a war zone, to live in a place that becomes defined by the battles and bloodshed. Vicksburg now conjures images of horrific carnage and people living in caves. No longer when we say *Vicksburg*, do we see the beautiful bluff city on the Mississippi River."

"I prayed day and night to find a way for the unionists and secessionists to work through their interpretations of the Constitution and equally important, their egotistical and economic posturing, to find a way to address the legal posturing, but, John, ultimately, no man can own another man's soul. How could anyone ever think for one minute that enslaving men, women, and families was the way to build a country? It's our bleakest hour. And, the Reconstruction is going to be painfully slow and chaotic. Do you think that mankind will ever find a way to solve its differences without war? What's the saying, '*Blood is thicker than water*'? I've always understood that saying to mean that the relationship with family is the most important thing. I found this war split families, and many died on both sides, splintered from their family's core. I know this behavior isn't new. I've heard stories from my mother's family that her relatives fought as patriots of this country and as British Loyalists during the American Revolution."

"Kate, families have fought since Cain and Abel."

"Yes, but we act like they shouldn't, then go right ahead with 'fight to the death' mantras. Surely, we're intelligent enough and have hearts that want peace and honor badly enough that we could create a better way to work through our differences. We're at our worst when we allow jealousy, greed, fear of something different than ourselves, desire to control everything around us as our motivators."

"You know it's not that simple."

"It's that simple. We complicate it, John. Let's go back to the African, Samuel. Didn't you have a different opinion of him after you had a conversation with him? Didn't you see that he wanted the same thing you wanted—a home to raise a family and to live in peace with prosperity?"

"You're right about my opinion of Samuel Blithers; it did change. But, Kate, don't think I hate all Africans, and hate is a strong word. I've known some good men and women too that I'd trust with my life. I think they need to know their place."

"Their place? Their place is not what you assign it. Their place is what they desire. Don't worry. I'm pretty sure they don't want your place. Because a person didn't grow up in the same culture or have the same color skin, doesn't mean that they're less than another; they're simply different. It's our cultural beliefs that we hold so dear, and they are going to kill us in the end."

"There has always been slavery. The Bible teaches us dominance of the chosen people over others."

"I'm not a Bible expert, but I can say this, you don't see dominance in the New Testament. If you believe in the crucifixion of Jesus Christ in a literal or in a philosophical sense, you must see the change. If we can't see the shift in the world, the call to shift our culture, then we truly are doomed. Constructing our world from Old Testament stories is far from the answer."

"The Bible is the Bible, Kate. It's the inspired word of God."

"I believe that I've already spoken to that point, John. When a person realizes that practice, policy, and ideology are wrong, you'd think that that realization would kick the door open, so to speak, for some universal application. You know, when you saw Samuel as a man, not a means, everything changed."

"What are you talking about and how did you get to the unique perspectives that you have?"

"They aren't unique; they're suppressed, but not unique. Most everything we know of the world, we know through the filter of men who want control and power over everything. My perspective comes, in part, from being a lifelong friend of Notch's. I've been in earshot of both sides of the discussion about the relocation of the Indians."

"As a child, I'd hear conversations describing the Indian people, and the negative descriptions that I heard weren't at all what I knew of the Indian folks that I knew/know. Something wasn't right; the story was skewed and skewed badly. Some things were just simply misunderstood. Why, for goodness sake, did we, the United States, need to relocate anyone? There's enough land for all of us. And John, once you can say that this treatment is wrong for a group of people, then we must know that it's wrong for every group of people. No one can truly believe that enslaving the Africans was the right thing to do. No one, not even the slavers of hundreds of years ago. I know that I'm about to step on your beliefs, but those people who use the Bible to defend slavery are just weak. I know that slavery existed in Biblical times, but just because it existed doesn't make it right. The story doesn't end there."

"Hang on, Kate, when you start talking about the Bible, I've got to step in. The Bible is the Word of the Lord. It's infallible. What it says is what goes."

"The Bible is a collection and selection, I might add, of information that was written over hundreds of years and may well have been inspired by a higher power, but was also filtered through the minds of males, who quite frankly, I think, had no idea how ubiquitous God is and consequently limit the Power of the Almighty. "

"Ubiquitous, what do you mean?"

"I mean ever-present, far-reaching. What I'm saying is that the inspiration was filtered through the current context of the writer's experience. How could they not be limited? Those men weren't God. They weren't ubiquitous. They could only write how they could relate to the inspiration. And, then, of course, you have additional layers of interpretation based on translators, who may or may not understand the concept that was intended by a word or groups of words and phrases that perhaps didn't even exist in the language to which the words were being transcribed. Therefore, the transcribers were also limited in their ability to translate based on their limited perceptions of the world."

"This line of thought of yours troubles me, Kate. The Bible is the divine word of God."

Kate realized that her voice was getting impassioned. She also knew she wasn't going to change John's mind, but she couldn't help herself. "If Jesus came to change the world, then a whole lot more emphasis should be put on the New Testament as opposed to the

Old Testament. I don't think you'll find, anywhere, where Jesus says if you're stronger and more powerful, then enslave people. 'Whip them into compliance.' Split families—wives and children from their husbands and fathers—change their names. It's not there."

There was a brief silence between the two of them.

"Then there's me. What are you going to do with me, John?" Since they'd become intimate, the space between the two of them was relaxed and always open to playfulness.

His blue eyes smiled, and he said, "I know what I'd like to do with you."

Kate feigned a smirk. "I had the great privilege of hearing Sarah Margaret Fuller speak before I left the Institute. Now, that was a woman on fire! At one time, she was considered the most well-read person, not a woman, mind you, but a person, in all of New England. She was an advocate for women's education and believed that once women were educated at equal levels to men, then they should have equal political rights. John, do you know how it weighs on me that I can't vote in an election in the United States or the great state of Mississippi?"

"Oh my! She wants to vote!"

"Well, of course, I do, and you'd be smart not to tease too much on this front. "

"Kate, politics, and voting—those things are very complicated, and I don't mean complicated as in you wouldn't understand it, but I think most women would like to be protected from it."

"Most women would like to have a voice in the policies that shape their lives. Who wouldn't? Do you want people making decisions for you?" She rushed ahead not giving him time to answer, "Think about it. Anyway, Sarah Margaret Fuller believed that women could be anything they wanted if they had an affinity for it, even a sea captain! Would you have boarded the *Isabella* if you had known that the captain was a woman?"

"That's an interesting question."

She didn't press him for an answer but pushed forward with her thoughts. "Fuller admitted that she'd been brought up to think that the Indians were unruly and refused to be civilized, but on a trip out West, she came to the very different conclusion that the

Indians had been treated very unfairly. This is not so unlike your interaction with Samuel Blithers. She supported the rights of Negroes and called on all abolitionists to also stand up against restrictions that suppressed women. You see, it's all connected John, it's all connected, and these connections create a better plan for moving forward than the suppression and subjugation that has been and is taking place in our societies now."

She went on to say that Fuller had written a book that could change the world as they knew it. It was called, *Women in the Nineteenth Century.* "The book gave me permission, or maybe encouragement is a better word, to pursue my own 'perspective' as you call it. Reading it was an affirmation to me that there's validity in my seeing things differently from what this or that organized group or even individuals may be promulgating. Do you know that she was the first woman allowed to use the library at Harvard College?"

"You don't say!"

"Now, why would anyone be denied access to a library, to reading, to a wealth of ideas?"

"Is this woman Christian?"

"She appears to have a deep faith in God, but I don't know much about her thoughts on religion. I understand that she was a member of the Unitarian Church, at least marginally."

"Was she married? And, what happened to her? You talk about her as a woman of the past."

"I forgot to mention that Margaret was the first female editor of the *New York Tribune*. She was a beautiful woman with long dark brown hair that trailed loosely down her back. She had large dark eyes and soft facial features. She wasn't married, but she had a daughter with an Italian, Giovanni Ossoli. She met him when she worked as a correspondent for the *Tribune*. The entire family died tragically in a shipwreck off Fire Island, New York as they were returning to the United States from abroad. She was 40 years old."

"Well, Kate, I can't say that I agree with everything you're saying, but you're a very smart woman. I don't think it's right for this woman to have a child out of wedlock. Why didn't she marry this Ossoli fellow?"

"So, just where do you draw the lines, John?"

He just looked at her, speechless, and she continued, "Let's have some dinner. How about the left-over rice with over easy eggs?"

"My favorite."

Kate was a bit of a paradox. She could be very quiet for extended periods of time, and not from depression or sadness. John teased her, saying that although she was quiet, he knew she was thinking about something. At other times she could talk for hours. John was never sure which Kate he would encounter on any given day, but he loved them both and would meet her in whatever state she was.

After supper as the two snuggled under the quilt that Kate had brought with her belongings from home, she asked, "Did you ever visit the sea, the Gulf?"

"No, not really. Not for recreational purposes if that's what you mean. I've had business to conduct at the actual port in Mobile. The folks in the general area had a lot of trepidation about hurricanes and such, but my place at Yellow Pine is far enough inland that it has generally not been affected by ocean storms. I never really gave it much thought until now. You cause me to consider so many things I've never given thought to before."

"The storms can be fierce, make you know just how small you are in the scheme of things — the universe. And, yes, I remember the storms of 1860. What a year! Three storms along the Gulf Coast in one year and others on the East Coast. Jake and I had only been married a few months, and I was new at living in proximity to the coast. Two of the storms were very memorable."

"The first was on August 12. It came ashore along the way between Biloxi and Pascagoula. It was a wide storm, and even though it moved off to the east, the strong winds and heavy rains battered New Orleans. They said over 60 people died, but I heard later reports that fishermen might not have been able to find refuge. The second hit a month and two days later, on September 14. It wrecked a tiny fishing town in Louisiana named Bazile. *The Times-Picayune* said that some people waded out in shoulder-high water and that the strong winds pushed the steamer *Galveston* ashore. The newspaper went on to profile both storms, which were of similar intensity, but the condition of the soil and water was different for each storm."

"The condition was described something like this. For the August storm the swamps were nearly dry which provided the lake with a natural release, but in September the swamps were so full that there was no place for the water to go; consequently, it flooded for quite a distance inland, even covering the railroad tracks, but really that was small news compared to what happened next in Biloxi. The ocean waves came in at 20 to 30 feet, the lighthouse was washed into the Gulf, and a hotel collapsed. Folks in Pascagoula said that the sea rose higher than they'd seen it in 40 years."

"Oh yes, I do remember that mess. Mobile took a beating from that second storm in September. They said the water rose seven feet in 20 minutes. In addition to losing the cotton crop in the fields, the storage barns along the wharves were flooded, and all the cotton that was stored there was lost as well."

"Bad times. I asked about the hurricane season in Brazil. Get this! They don't have one. The old gentleman that buys my flowers for the market said that there's only been one hurricane in anyone's memory in Brazil. I think you should put that little piece of information in your scouting report to tell the folks back home!"

"You may have a point there, young lady!"

"Don't you think it's amazing how the ocean holds within itself the most remarkable, divergent temperament? You can feel it coming, can't you? The storm, I mean."

"Yes, like they say, the calm before the storm."

"A certain warning of something volatile to come. That stillness evokes an almost trance-like state. It's just a bit eerie, don't you, think?"

"The quality of the air changes."

"I remember very clearly that first summer near the coast, seeing low gray clouds sliding across the smoke colored sky like shifting ice plates, moving southwest from the north, indicating we were in the outer rim of the storm's spin."

She drew a deep breath, "As I said earlier, the ocean has such a different temperament. Outside of the storms, I've always enjoyed walking along the beach. Before the war, my husband had some construction work to do in Pass Christian. At that time, it was becoming quite the resort town with second homes and villas of the wealthy from New Orleans, the cotton and cane plantations. I'd accompany him on his travels there, and before he'd go off to whatever appointment or analysis he had to do, he'd set up a lean-to on the beach so that I could hide from the sun. I'd bring a hefty book and sitting and reading, listening to the constant rhythm of the waves. The truth of the matter was that Jake was always back too soon. I could listen to the waves all day. I found it exhilarating to sit under the vastness of blue skies at the edge of the ocean, looking out past the barrier islands into the blue-green watery infinity — such a speck of humanity. How grand we are to be able to grasp such awareness. How minuscule we are in comparison."

John propped up on his elbow to see her face better and with the back of his hand wiped a wisp of hair from her eyes. "Perhaps we could take the train to Santos and see the ocean there. I'd like to see it with your eyes. Would you like that?"

"Yes, let's do. I think Costa Verde is the place to go. I've heard there are orchids growing all around and white sand beaches like the ones along the U.S. Gulf Coast back home. They say the Verde Mountains drop directly into a calm azure sea. Locally they refer to this area as the Atlantic Rain Forest, Yes, let's go!"

She smiled and began drifting off to sleep as she imagined wading in the Atlantic Ocean, nearly 5,000 miles from where she'd away. She wondered if the water would be warm.

Kate reeled in her physical relationship with John. Such delight was something she had thought she might not have known again. The intensity, playfulness, and desperation ignited her senses and made her days more vivid than the color of the blue finch that nestled in the rosemary garden while she tasted her morning coffee, and the softness of the loosed strands of hair that blew across her face. But she truly cherished the intimacy of conversation — an echo of her earlier life, the closeness of another body warm, next to hers in the night, his hand at her lower back as he guided her through doorways and across streets.

As John sliced the watermelon he had brought from the nearby stream where he'd been cooling it for two days, Kate asked, "Have you ever had your picture taken?"

"No."

"I think we should do that, have our picture taken together, it's becoming such a common thing."

"Yes, it's becoming quite the profession—making photography something that is more available to the common person—but I haven't seen any photographers in São Paulo. Have you?"

"No, but I bet this place will be crawling with them as more southerners move down here."

"I wonder what photography will do for memory," Kate mused.

"Oh, hold on, I can tell you have been thinking about this, haven't you?"

"Well, isn't it interesting how different people remember shared experiences? What do you think photography will do for those recollections?" Kate took a deep breath but didn't give John time to answer, "You know, you'll have a memory of some past incident, you meet someone who shared the experience, and they don't remember what you remember at all, but they may have some additional impression of the happening that they share. I think that is fascinating. I don't understand it. I suppose we remember the aspect of the incident that was most important to us as an individual, but I must say that line of thinking doesn't seem to play out consistently. Do you think we lack the capacity for a full memory? Each person's memory is their truth of the incident, but rarely does anyone hold the whole truth. I'm intrigued by individual perception. Sometimes memory comes in glimpses or flashes. From my childhood, I remember fields of broomsedge in the sunlight. What was it used for? Why do I remember just that—no sounds, no people surrounding it? And, what is that color that is so hard to name? I do know that I belong to a 'tribe' that swept dirt!" She laughed.

"Tribe, what? Please elaborate on that last comment."

"I remember my mother telling me that there was no grass growing in front of the four or five steps that led into her home. My mother would sweep the sandy area with broom sedge brooms—

the broomsedge was tied in bundles with a strip of cloth torn from something, an old cleaning cloth—something old and very worn out. The three ties were spaced about four or five inches apart at the top third of the stalks, leaving the feathery bottom parts to act as a broom. After my mother swept, her sister would come around, evaluate the job, and consequently, always sweep again. My mother wasn't the perfectionist that my aunt was, but in the case of sweeping sand, I think that is perfectly acceptable. How perfect does swept sand need to be?"

"That's a funny story. I do know broom sedge as well, grows in pasture land, where for the most part the soil is worn out. I haven't spent so much time as you in thinking about other people's perspectives. I've got to say, as for me, well, my opinion, or perspective as you call it, is the right one." He chuckled.

She smiled. "I know, John, and it more than amazes me that your steadfast opinions don't frustrate me more than they do."

"That's a good thing."

"About the photography, you know this war is the first to be so fully captured by photography as a means of reporting the news." He glanced at Kate, and continued, "I read that over 750 photographers took pictures of all sorts of war-related events, including battlefields scattered with corpses. I have mixed feelings about showing dead soldiers scattered about; it seems disrespectful to the dead and their loved ones, but I guess one thing it does is help the people calling the shots, literally—the officials—to understand the consequence of war. "

"It has been a hard thing to see."

"We're about at the four-year anniversary of the Battle of Antietam that took place right outside Sharpsburg, Maryland. The numbers of casualties from that battle are astounding. I heard the numbers were in the thousands, Kate, thousands—something like 3,700 killed, 17,000 wounded. It was a bloody day indeed. It's a wonder that such loss didn't culminate an end to the war right there, but it continued two more long years." His voice began to trail, "You know the sound of a bullet hitting flesh sounds different from any other sound. It makes a plinking sound, like something hitting the water—gunshots hitting flesh. When I see those photographs of the Battle of Antietam, the visual is amplified by the multiplied plinking sound of flesh exploding." John didn't elaborate on how he knew such a thing, but continued, "I suspect that photography will be used to help us to savor memories and to report current events more vividly, but as you say, perspective, previous experience, will always play some role in interpreting what the photograph reveals."

On a bright Saturday morning, John and Kate headed to one of their favorite places, the triangular park in the city's center. As they walked, they didn't hold hands, but the inside of their open palms rubbed together, her left inside his right, barely touching. They did some window shopping along the way, sometimes briefly stepping inside a shop. He watched her look at decorative coffee cups with tiny saucers. When he asked her which one she liked best, she didn't hesitate to say "the set with the wild blackberries." He immediately took the collection to the register and had it wrapped carefully for her; the first thing he had ever bought for her. Almost as quickly as they stepped outside, John stepped into a tiny café to purchase a cup of coffee for each of them. He was deeply engaged in placing the order when he turned quickly to her and asked in a languid, punctuated manner, "Do you want cream in your coffee?"

Kate burst out laughing. "John, you and I, we speak the same language." He looked at her a bit stunned, and after a couple of seconds, he realized what he'd done. He reached over and grabbed her up in a tight hug and laughed, "I love you, Kate Teal."

"Yes, I'd like coffee, *preto*, please. Black," she said.

As they sat drinking their coffee, Kate continued, "All of these options for tea seem quite unusual to me."

"I know, seems very British, but tea was offered to us throughout the scouting tour. Sometimes it was offered to us in a gourd, and it didn't always taste like tea to me. I'm a traditionalist, you know."

"Tea served up in a gourd is an ancient tradition from the indigenous people of the area. What kind of traditionalist are you?"

He smiled at her, "You know, damn well what I mean."

She laughed, "Yes, I do. I've found that you must be very careful asking for tea here. Sometimes it meets our definition of traditional, but often it's infused with other things. Pineapple is a popular additive. What you had in the gourd was probably *mate* or *yerba mate*, which was originally cultivated by the *Tupi* people. The *yerba mate*, which is translated *mate herb* looks a bit like mistletoe to me. You know mistletoe? The leaves of the *mate* are smoother, less dense, and it grows from an independent bush, and not as a parasitic growth high in trees. The tea is best made with very hot, but not boiling water. It troubles me that the traditional tea production for local use and export is heavily dependent on slave labor. I wonder how this country is going to resolve the issue of slavery?"

"I don't know, but frankly, I don't think it'll be too far in the future; even though in my travels, I didn't witness any significant unrest. It's just a premonition. I also think that this country will begin shifting more towards coffee production when they get all the variables right."

When they were settled on the park bench, John was the first to pose a question. "Kate, have you ever been to a circus?"

"No, I haven't, have you?"

"Yes. It's been a while, but I've been."

"I've seen sketches of trapeze artists and such."

"The shows are fantastic Kate. A circus came to Mobile a few years ago, and I happened to be in town, so I took it in. The various acts featured a husband and wife team of tightrope walkers. Their sense of balance was nothing short of miraculous. I found myself holding my breath as they made their way across the high top of the big tent. You could see the concentration on their faces as they went from one side of the wire to the other. They were both fit, and that young woman had plenty of nerve. I'll never forget what a spectacle they were. Both were wearing shiny royal blue tops. She had red and blue feathers worked into her hair. Then, the bareback riders, well they were something else. There was one guy who was supposed to be the greatest equestrian in the world—a big word for a sawmill guy, right?" John winked.

"You know that's how they advertise these events—the biggest, the tallest, the most treacherous, and so on." Kate smiled as John continued.

"This guy did 36 somersaults in a row! Now, how do you keep your balance doing that? The room has got to be spinning. He was indeed the somersault king! He did somersaults from a standing position on the back of the white horse to the floor. Then, after returning to the back of the horse and standing, he did a backward somersault on the horse's back while the horse trotted around the arena. Great entertainment, I tell you. Great."

"Were there any exotic animals with the troupe?"

"This particular exhibition didn't have animals, but remember the African fella I was telling you about—Sam Blithers? He told me that one night while the slavers were taking the Africans to their new owners, up around Selma, there was a party approaching from the south. The Africans were made to leave the road and make their way through the brush. As the group got closer, a low rumble of grunts and snorts could be heard. There was a lot of rattling, jingling, and talking. As the approaching group neared, it was evident that it was a traveling circus. About the time the circus was even with the Africans, a loud trumpeting blast burst out, something not human. The slavers were startled, but the Africans stopped in their tracks in disbelief. An elephant made the noise they heard. I expect the sight of an elephant at dusk along a packed red dirt road in Alabama was pretty shocking, but Blithers said it was comforting to his people—made them feel a little closer to home."

"My goodness! An elephant in Alabama! Had to be a sight." They both laughed, probably more than the story called for, but laughter was something that came naturally to them when they were together, as natural as breathing.

"When my uncle was a boy, he captured a monkey that was left behind by a circus visiting New Orleans."

"Tell me that story, Kate." John loved the sound of her voice and would often get her to tell stories he might not be exceedingly interested in, just loved to hear her talk and the emotion she brought to most anything she said.

She started with her head tilted just a bit to the left, as she often did, her blue eyes looking a little mischievous. "Well, this is the way my Uncle Benjamin tells the story, which I believe to be fully true. There'd be no reason not to believe my uncle." She laughed. "As the story goes, one day, Uncle Benjamin's sister, my Aunt Mary Anna, came storming into her parent's yard, kicking up dust as she came and yelled for the brother, she called *Brother*. Mary Anna, who was a petite, feisty-tempered brunette and had a reputation for saying what was on her mind, often just before she flashed a sensational, wide smile, lived next to my grandparents at the outskirts of the city of New Orleans. 'Brother! Brother! You've got to come get this thing! You've got to come get this thing! It's making a mess of my garden.'"

"Mary Anna shouted in a high-pitched exclamation that the offending "thing" was a monkey that had been left behind by the circus. It was going from row to row eating the onions in her garden. The challenge of catching a wayward monkey was right up Uncle Benjamin's alley. He was a young boy of 13 or 14 at the time. He jumped on a rickety old bicycle he shared with his brothers and was on the hunt. He was beaten to the garden by a bunch of coon dogs that were baying at the monkey they'd treed at the edge of Mary Anna's garden. About the time Uncle Benjamin made eye contact with the frightening, shivering little monkey, it leaped from the magnolia tree right into his arms!" Kate couldn't help laughing at the story every time she heard or told it as she imagined her Uncle Benjamin's surprise when he found himself holding a circus monkey.

"Well, what in the world did your uncle do with a circus monkey?"

"The story gets a little sketchy at this point, but it seems as though my uncle secured the monkey at a ready-made furniture store in town. The owner of the store somehow came to believe that the monkey belonged to him. The owner thought displaying a live monkey might bring in more business. Benjamin felt that since he'd captured the monkey or had been captured by him, whichever the case was, that the monkey belonged to him. He convinced the storekeeper to let him bring the monkey home to show his mother. It appears there was a delay in bringing the monkey back to the store. Uncle Benjamin says he never told the man he was bringing the monkey back. For safekeeping, Benjamin and one of his cousins, who lived a mile or so away from my grandparents, rotated keeping the monkey under the pretense that changing the location regularly, would make it more difficult for anyone who might be looking to claim it." Kate took a deep breath and sighed, "Benjamin says that his cousin told him the monkey ran away, but Uncle Benjamin thinks he sold it."

"Now, I don't care who you are, that's funny!"

"Maybe, for you, but not for my Uncle Benjamin!"

"Did I tell you we heard monkeys while we were on the first leg of the expedition?" They both began to laugh uncontrollably, which shifted into a night of jovial lovemaking. Across their Brazilian coffee the next morning, the laughter started again. Neither of them could ever remember when they'd been so undeniably happy.

Kate loved his energy. She wouldn't allow him to refer to himself as an old man. She thrived on his affirmation of her and felt that he needed someone to accept him fully—flaws and all. She was capable of such love. He professed a great love for her, and she believed he was sincere, but she would've been lying if she'd said she thought he'd stay with her. She admitted that she hoped beyond all hope for it, but she knew, in the end, he wouldn't. She never thought of their relationship ending when they were together. The joy, the indulgent laughter, was always there between the two of them. The laughter was like breathing, and they lived for every breath together. There was no doubt about the mutuality of their feelings. Kate was aware that the calendar wasn't her friend, but she kept those thoughts buried as best she could.

Before they realized it, darkness had draped across the park hastily and encompassed the town. John and Kate meandered through the streets in the direction of Kate's cottage, taking an alleyway or two along the way to save a bit of time.

Suddenly, John grabbed Kate's arm and abruptly pushed her aside, causing her almost to lose her balance. As she was about to exclaim, she noticed the worried expression on his face and looked down. He had pushed her to prevent her from stepping in a large puddle of blood. He looked in every direction, pulled her close, and they walked quickly and quietly for the rest of the way.

"Blood pooled like that is the result of a gut wound. Don't ask me how I know," John said. "Kate, promise me that you will restrict your ramblings through this town to early daylight hours. Everything here is not sweet and kind the way you see it." Whether it was a divergent or related thought, Kate never knew, but he went on to say, "You know the majority of the southerners interested in coming here are looking to replicate an agrarian culture reliant on slave labor. I think that's a big mistake, a really big mistake."

During the evening, John was quieter than usual. As he pulled the quilt over them and settled into bed, Kate gave a little smile and placed the tip of her index finger on the bridge of his nose, noticing how the slight arch at the end of her finger filled the curve precisely. She thought that this was just another way that they fit together perfectly. She propped herself up on her elbow and kissed him lightly on his forehead and again where the curve of her finger had rested. He reciprocated with a lingering kiss to her forehead.

"All day, I've been thinking of an hourglass, you know, the ones with sand that pours from a higher bulb to a lower bulb. I'm not exactly sure of the complexities that contribute to the way the mechanism works—the density of the sand, the diameter of the opening between the bulbs, but they've been around for hundreds of years and are accurate. Anyway, I'm having a hard time getting the image out of my mind. I'm a steady fellow, Kate, but this image of the hourglass stays in mind, haunts me. Time is running out. Time is running out, and I can see it with my own two eyes."

She held him tighter and whispered, "We're here now. You hold my beating heart in our hands."

The next morning over *chá preto quente*, as she loved to say, he made a simple comment that he intended as an accolade, "You're a strong woman Lillian Kate Teal. You *are* a strong woman."

She looked directly into his searching blue eyes, knowing that he thought there was a compliment in his words. "Yes, because I must be, and I know I'll be punished for my strength. Because I can be strong doesn't mean that I should always have to be." She tied on her gardening apron and headed to the patch of new green vegetables where she relentlessly pulled the weeds that had sprouted, then pinched the fading blooms.

BEGINNING AGAIN

Salt Water

As John began to tell Kate the story of a leaf he'd watched floating down a stream, her heartbeat slowed, and she realized she was barely breathing as she listened. He looked across the room as he spoke, and he seemed distant. He was not aware of the fact that he'd told her this story before; however, this time, his perspective of the experience had changed dramatically. Kate listened without moving a muscle.

"A while back, I sat on the bank of a river and watched a leaf float downstream. I don't know how long I sat there, but it seemed like quite some time. I watched that leaf, Kate, carried by the water's current from one side of the shallow riverbed to the other, pushed over and around rocks, brushing against clumps of leaves gathered against the side of the bank, being pushed around rocks, floating gently downstream, until it was completely out of sight. A single leaf was caught up in the current like it had no purpose. It was alone, separated from all the other leaves. I felt so sad for it floating all alone."

Kate didn't say a word. She knew, whether he did or not that he was projecting his feelings on the leaf, and his original perception of that leaf as an independent life force, experiencing life to its fullest was gone as if he had never told the story before. He didn't remember his mythology. She felt helpless and angry and resolved not to share her reaction to the story, but to accept it as best she could. Over the past weeks she'd convinced herself that somehow, he'd work out living his life with her, but now she knew he wouldn't, he couldn't stay the course. He couldn't make such a dramatic change. She understood his keen sense of responsibility to his family, but she also knew that what existed between them was rare, and in her mind was worth trying to find a way to save. It was difficult to accept him walking away from what was so vital to her.

Kate had not accompanied him any further than her front door the day he left her.

On the return voyage back to the United States, John craved Kate; he couldn't wait to return to her. He would figure out a way to be with her and was resolute that he would not have to give her up.

Dawn was her most contemplative time as she absorbed the grief of losing what she'd wanted so badly.

Morning light seeped in slowly as she tried to rouse herself, but the bed seemed to be the best place. She lay there thinking of all the prayers that needed saying, all the while feeling the blood pulsing too fast in her left temple as if to wake a wretched headache. She couldn't fathom what was so important that she must leave her perfect bed where the previous day's sadness sloughed off through the night, and the rest caused her to feel more like herself. The early morning quiet, the stillness that existed even before the birds sang and the cat cried to get out—the scene in its totality was a soothing thing.

The yellow, dappled light seeped across her pillow and reflected off the silver in the bracelet that she wore around her slender wrist. Her breathing was even and deep. She was merely present in the moment, aware of the way her right foot lay on the left, cradled in the arch, aware that the mockingbird had started chirping outside her window. She'd savor this peace as long as she could and hesitated to move at all. When she did turn and stretch her legs across the cool cotton sheets, she knew it was time to face a new day that held the same questions.

The day started with irritation that here she was again, not knowing which step to take next. Falling in love with John had startled her awake, like the sudden sight of a red male cardinal in a vibrant green, rain-drenched summer afternoon. Losing him had left her emotionally immobilized, dull in every way. As she watched a little brown thrush, she thought of Charles Darwin's evolution theory and felt that maybe humans hadn't come so far after all. The little bird knew precisely where it was supposed to be and what it was supposed to be doing. She wondered what evolutionary trait she'd lost, or missed entirely, that would keep her on a steady path.

Kate had always sought refuge and comfort in her gardening, so she went about readying her plots for the Brazilian spring. Her cool crops, the bunches of dark green turnip leaves were growing well. She enjoyed the turnip leaves cooked down until they were tender, hopefully with ham hocks. She remembered how her grandmother used to fuss about having to wash the turnips repeatedly to get the sand off the leaves. As she padded around pulling the turnip leaves, she remembered a delightful soup she'd once had at a dinner when she was at the Institute. It was made from the root of the turnip and pears. She wondered if she could re-create the soup or come close to it anyway. She'd not seen pears in Brazil, perhaps she could find a substitute, but an alternative would be *feijoada*, a black bean stew with smoked sausage, to compliment the turnips.

Given her need for a task on which she could focus, her spring garden was looking splendid, and this observation gave her comfort. In the garden, she felt fully present like she felt at almost no other time. It was a presence that took her breath away like a ruby-throated hummingbird darting past. The squash plants were growing, tomatoes were sturdy, cucumber vines had begun to creep around and would need stakes and netting soon, potato tops were looking strong, and green onions were ready for cutting. Kate loved the smell of green onions being chopped. Her rosemary had lasted through the mild winter, as had the Spanish lavender. She cut a handful of the fragrant herbs that mixed to make a divine scent, thinking she'd put them in a bit of water beside her bed after she made her nightly cup of *chá quente*. She scattered tiny pieces of lavender languidly as she went, leaving behind a thistle colored sunset as she made her way into the house.

As the days went by, she fell into a routine, assisting with general tasks around the school, preparing to teach the children of the *Confederados*, and continuing to learn to make local dishes for her meals. From time to time she'd find a scrap of paper where John had scribbled the word *still*. He had left the notes in unsuspecting places throughout her tiny house—under a seldom-used coffee cup stored at the back of the kitchen cabinet, tucked between pages of a favorite book, in her walking boots. She stopped breathing every time she discovered a note. The awareness of how much she loved him rushed through her, something she never forgot, but on most days, could keep in some intellectual containment until the notes appeared, always with just the one word *still*. She knew the notes were meant to comfort her and remind her of his love, but they also reminded her of how he'd gone away, and she couldn't realistically expect ever to see him again.

Alfonso, the groundskeeper, was aware of the loss and he'd become vigilant about working on the cottage property on a regular basis. Kate had been very kind to him, and he seemed to feel it was essential to keep an eye out for her in this time of distress, which was easy enough as Kate had begun to call on him more and more as a resource for her kitchen garden. She found that he understood English better than he could speak it. The understanding was beneficial to her as she wasn't yet familiar with the soil and the difference in the varieties of plants.

One afternoon when she was busy fussing over a profusion of pink and purple bougainvillea, Alfonso brought a map to Kate and asked her to show him where she came from. She opened the map and first located Rio de Janeiro and Santos. Using those bearings, she then pointed out the approximate location of São Paulo. Next, she slid her index finger northward through the Atlantic Ocean and pointed to the southern United States Gulf, specifically the Mississippi Gulf Coast and a bit inland. Her eyes filled with tears. Alfonso smiled at her and said, "The ocean has too much *água salgada*." She patted the pool of tears forming in her eyes, laughed and admitted, "Yes, it does." At that moment an awareness came over her that she'd never cross the ocean back to Mississippi. She had made her own home.

Her thoughts shifted to John. She was astonished that the two of them had lived so near each other all their lives but had never met until the voyage. She wondered if their paths had ever crossed, perhaps in Mobile.

"Alfonso, I've found that hope lives in the heart and is a hard thing to kill off." She continued to speak as if working her way through a puzzle. "The New England writer Emily Dickinson says that 'hope is a thing with feathers.' I'm not sure that I understand what she means. I think that hope has many different qualities. Hope is a warrior, an ember in the eternal flame. Hope is tenacious and holds when everything logical and rational dies away. Alfonso, where do you think the line is that distinguishes hope from denial?"

"I believe it's where the truth is, ma'am."

"What is the truth?"

"The truth is what is possible."

"Hmm, that was a good try Alfonso," Her voice began to falter. "I find most anything, and everything is possible, perhaps not probable, but possible."

As she allowed her mind to flood with memories, she reflected on the reputation that women have for being mysterious; she now understood that women hold a lifetime of private images, most of which they never speak.

Alabama Sawmill (November 1866)

After experiencing his family's joy at his return home to Yellow Pine and subsequently their disappointment that he'd left at all, a heavy heartbreak seeped into the very air he breathed, Cynthia's cynical prattle and disdain for anything other than digging her heels in where she was, had infiltrated all their thinking. Not one glimmer of what might be possible in a new country emitted from his daughters or son-in-law, and certainly not from Cynthia.

As the Indian summer folded one day into another, John's concerns about the move to Brazil loomed larger and larger. He was genuinely skeptical about whether Emperor Dom Pedro II and the local governing authorities, who had been so hospitable, would be able to come through with the road infrastructure they had promised. Roads were critical to the success of every industry; but mostly, while he knew some of the men in the expedition saw slavery in Brazil as an asset to their agricultural aspirations, he felt trouble loomed ahead.

If the institution of slavery crumbled in America, how could it flourish in what he deemed to be lesser countries? He anticipated civil unrest and eventually war, which he never wanted to experience again. He could not fathom losing another family member to the violence of war. Even though he did not personally experience any unrest while he traveled, he felt the opportunity for war was not far away, with not only a potential uprising of the African slaves, but also the indigenous population that was enslaved. John thought an internal war in Brazil would be even more complicated than the one in the United States.

John began having dreams of his son's death, of his home burning, fear, and scarcity that deeply disturbed his sleep. His days were filled with efforts to deconstruct the dreams. He was more than concerned for Kate's well-being, and although he seldom compared the two women in any manner, he knew that Kate was as adamant about a fresh start as Cynthia was about staying in place.

He knew she did not sense the impending perils the way he did. He wished he could travel back to São Paulo and bring her home, but not only was the voyage impossible, but he also had no home to offer her. With that said, it was still difficult for him to get over the urge to write to her and beg her to come home. As the days went by, he became more and more reconciled to the fact that there was no way he could take care of her the way he wanted.

As John stood a few feet from the back steps of his home surveying the dilapidation that had occurred over the past years. He lightly brushed the brittle, brown crumbling leaves side to side with his right foot, reaching down, now and then, to pick up a pecan or two, perfect in their oblong shape and larger this year, full of golden brown nut meat. He had been mindlessly cracking the dark brown shells, one against the other, breaking the two halves apart and removing the thin layer of dark red bitter from the meat before he popped it in his mouth. John thoroughly enjoyed the subtle taste of pecans. He was glad that even though the pecans on the ground beneath the trees had been regularly picked up and bagged for selling, a few stragglers remained for his indulgence.

He remembered as a child one of his responsibilities had been cracking and cleaning more pecans than he cared to think about for his mother's Christmas baking. The task was made bearable because he became very good at sneaking pieces for consumption. His tongue was always chasing a bit here or there against his teeth, trying to keep his mouth clear so he wouldn't have to hear his mother say, "John Bailey Foster, are you eating more pecans than you're saving for my Christmas pies?" He could never stop eating the finished product, pecan pie, until he was on the verge of being sick from its sweetness—the jelly-like center made of egg yolk and sugar with a hard-baked layer of pecan halves on top, all cradled in a perfect pie crust, rim flattened with the tines of a fork. Oh, how he'd love to hear his mother's admonishments one more time.

John had just put six or eight pecans in his jacket pocket when he heard Cynthia slam the back door and start toward him. Could that woman walk out without slamming a door these days? As she pulled her heavy gray woolen shawl tightly against her, John thought that the day wasn't as cold as all that. He reached back into his pocket, pulling out two pecans and cracked the thin shells by squeezing them together in the palm of his hand. Cynthia's approach was slow but quite deliberate.

By the time she reached John, he'd cleaned both pecans and bid her open her palms where he lay the four perfect halves and smiled. With no comment, she ate the pecans then said, "They have been good and plentiful this year, which is a good thing with so much else failing around us. The few dollars that have come in from the sale of the orchard pecans is something."

Usually, even a positive comment from Cynthia was laced with bitterness and gloom, or caution at best. Although John fully registered her attitude, he didn't acknowledge it. In part, it was the way he kept a high opinion of her. He'd disregard the parts of her personality that were less attractive. He kept all that belonged to him, so to speak, at its highest level of perfection, at least in his mind.

He smiled sincerely, "I've come home to you before the holidays, just as I promised I'd do."

"Yes, you have come home John. Home, where you belong — where your responsibility to this family, myself included, is. But I can tell you aren't settled. I've heard your stories of your lush Brazil. You and your starry-eyed idea of creating a New South in Brazil, but THIS is your responsibility John — this farm and sawmill, this town and this state for that matter. It's your job to work to retrieve what has been lost and restore proper order. You can change things for the better if you would just put your selfishness aside. You're such the dreamer. Always have been. Be realistic."

"Cynthia, did you hear the part where I said, despite all the good that I saw, I didn't think a move to Brazil was worth the financial investment. Cotton growing hasn't been perfected in the southern regions where the incentives are, coffee cultivation is in its infancy, but mainly, transportation resources across the country and to neighboring countries are vastly limited, stifling trade. The Brazilian government has promised more, but I don't see that coming to fruition." He chose not to even broach the issue of slavery with her.

Here was her chance to say, which she seldom missed, "I told you so."

John knew that, even given the badgering, he couldn't live without his family. He set about to rebuild his livelihood. Within the next couple of years, he built the sawmill into a business of significant impact. During this time, raw timber could be purchased for $3 to $5 per thousand board feet and then sold as lumber for $10 - $15 per thousand board feet. Transportation down the river was easier than ever and still cost efficient.

John had the sawmill working and was invested in the rearing of his grandchildren; however, with all that he had, there was a place in his heart that sometimes expanded to engulf him when he thought of Kate. He knew she felt it was easy for him to leave her, but that was the furthest notion from the truth. He had written her to try to explain all that he was responsible for, but of course, she didn't, couldn't respond. He wondered if she received his letters. He wondered what she thought of them. He wondered if she had yet found all the notes he'd left behind to let her know his feelings for her were indeed real. Yes, he thought of her often —when he looked at the moon, when he heard the first bird chirp early in the morning, when he looked across the Dog River, when he inhaled.

String of Pearls

Kate had grown accustomed to giving up things, which over the years had caused her to need little in the way of material things, but occasionally something presented itself as irresistible.

Needing to transcend beyond the fog that was encompassing her thinking about her last conversation with John, Kate found herself strolling in and out of shops that lined the center of the city, which was the area in which she'd shopped when she first came to São Paulo. While she wasn't comfortable in crowds, the slow pace of a Saturday afternoon was perfect for meandering through the colors and textures and shapes in everything from furniture and drapery to porcelain china and jewelry. It was the latter she was unable to resist. At a much earlier occasion in her life, Kate had searched for the perfect pearl necklace, one that fit lightly at the base of her neck. She'd imagined it as the ideal timeless accessory. In recent years, until this very afternoon, she'd forgotten that pursuit. It had become lost in living.

When the string of pearls caught her eyes, everything else fell away. Her entire focus was on the necklace. The milky white beads lay in three short strands, one just a bit longer than the next and while the pearls themselves were lovely, it was the double clasp that drew her nearer the display case. The clasps were custom-cast silver pods, replicas of North American Lotus pods. The designer, a woman from Louisiana, left a note that revealed her inspiration which read, "In Asia, lotus flowers rising from the swamp symbolize the spirit's ability to bloom in any circumstance." She went on to say that she'd used the North American lotus pod to portray the essence of the human spirit to rise above adversity and flower. We all find our way through crises in different ways, Kate thought. As the jeweler had worked through her transition by creating the necklace, the completed design and story spoke directly to Kate's sense of beauty, but also reflected her penchant for hope, of which even she sometimes needed to be reminded. The necklace, she thought, was an outward sign, a response to a prayer she'd prayed for months for a healed heart. And, at that moment, her whole world shifted on a pearl necklace.

www.ingramcontent.com/pod-product-compliance
Lightning Source LLC
Chambersburg PA
CBHW030327020726
47493CB00004B/1190